I'm Mortuary Girl

CATHLEEN ELLIS

Cover design by Launie Parry
Interior design by Brian Schwartz

ISBN: 978-1629672076
Library of Congress Control Number: 2021902296

YOUNG PEOPLE IN LOVE
IN THE HEARTLAND OF AMERICA

1

Near Christmas 2006

"Gran loves me."

Mandy patted her hand over her heart, smiled and looked up, above the congregation.

"She's with me now," she said in her clear and strong voice. "And gran, as you're gazing at us from wherever you are, all around are your students, present, and past."

Mandy stood there, in the center of the sanctuary, without using the sound system. She lifted her arms and moved them into an imaginary embrace of the students sitting in the front pews of St. Paul's Church.

"Want to join me in wishing Mrs. Overton a Merry Christmas?"

She watched the students nod to her.

"Merry Christmas, Mrs. Overton," they smiled, shouted out and began clapping.

Mandy joined in with the clapping, "Whatcha think, gran?" she whispered.

When the congregation grew quiet, Mandy gave them a quick verbal vision of who her gran was.

"Never give up on your dreams," she paused, "Gran told me. Enjoy this day, 'cause it's special, not like yesterday, or tomorrow; love, and live, and learn."

She gave a slight bow of her head and walked down the sanctuary steps to where her parents and brother sat. The celebration of gran's life continued.

8)

Mary Beth Overton died five days before. When she did not report to her third grade class at school, the principal called Jim Overton, her son. He found his mom in her bed, a serene appearance on her pretty face. The autopsy reported a massive heart attack, an MI.

Mandy asked her folks how she could help them. Her dad, especially, expressed a numbness, an inability to really think straight. Mandy's mom, Cindy, never got along very well with headstrong Mary Beth, so she remained silent, letting her husband take the lead. Her folks gave Mandy free rein to work with the mortuary on a reception and the minister on the church celebration.

She had her own key to her grandma's home. For years Mandy went home from school with her gran and stayed there until her folks picked her up from work. When she turned 12, she got the key and would walk to gran's after school. Then, at 13, she walked to her own home and stayed by herself until her parents came home.

Mandy let out a big sigh as she let herself into gran's home. She had two orders from her parents, pick out a favorite outfit for gran, so the mortuary could dress her for the open casket funeral.

The second, "Ick, stinky, stinky," she held her nose.

She emptied trash, starting with the garbage sack under the kitchen sink. Spoiled food from the frig went into the garbage. Mandy moved from room to room and took all the trash to the garage, where gran kept the trash can. The next day the Porttown trash service would come and the smells would be gone. Mandy opened the garage door and set the trash can out at the curb. Two neighbors approached her.

Jeannie, from next door, hugged Mandy, "If there's anything we can do, just let us know, please. We want to help, and we are so sorry about your grandmother."

Mandy felt the hug from Sophia, a neighbor from across the street.

"I'm with Jeannie, if there's anything, at all, let us know."

"There is," Mandy paused, then nodded, "you special neighbors, snow removal, if you can keep the sidewalks clear, that would be a huge help, until my family gets that figured out. And please bring up the trash can later tomorrow, set it to the side of the house, kinda out of direct view. We've stopped the newspaper and forwarded mail."

"I know it's too soon, but what about your grandmother's home?" Jeannie asked.

Mandy affirmed, "That's OK, it's not too soon. My folks, so much to deal with, pretty sure, it'll go up for sale, right away."

"In a sense, that'll be awful, your grandmother, she, well, an awesome neighbor, willing to help out, did help out, us too, several times, that we can remember," Sophia nodded.

Mandy's brown eyes darkened as the neighbors watched her lips thin, "Yeah, that'll really be beyond our control."

"We know that, honey, again, so sorry."

The neighbors hugged Mandy again and walked away. Back inside Mandy decided to keep the wreath up on the front door. She turned the heat down to 64 degrees on the thermostat in the hall. In the kitchen she opened the dishwasher and added dirty dishes from the sink and kitchen table. She started the dishwasher and cleared and wiped down all the counters.

Mandy felt tears choking her nose and throat as she went through the closet searching for that special outfit she wanted to see her grandma in. She found it, a poinsettia-red winter dress. She laid the dress out on the carpeted floor and found black heels to go with black hose, underwear, and a pretty silver star pin to finish off the dress. Mandy made her grandma's bed and laid the outfit on the bed, visualizing how everything would look on gran.

"Gran, you're such a pretty lady, such a special lady. Everyone'll see that."

Mandy felt her nose go wet, but her eyes stayed clear.

The special request from Mandy's parents was placement of the open casket at the foyer inside the church entrance. In that way folks who wanted to could have a chance to see Mary Beth before the celebration of her life began.

Mandy carried the red dress in its plastic wrap over her arm and the rest of the clothing in a bag. She searched the gray sky for signs of snow clouds as she walked the blocks to her own home.

"Nope, no snow yet."

"But, before long, Mandy," she heard her gran's voice.

Mandy turned, seeing her gran in her winter bright blue coat.

"Gran, oh Gran, you're with me."

She saw her gran smile and nod, "I am, and I'll always be, my memory, in your heart."

"You're going to God, to your new home."

"I am, my darling, it'll be some tough sledding, for you at times. I know you'll do something with your life to serve people."

"But I'm not sure what," she paused, "yet."

"Keep this thought with you always, Mandy, don't back down from who you are and what you want to be."

"Thank you, Gran, I'll remember that always, and one day I'll join you."

Mandy kept walking; she felt the warmth next to her fading. When she turned to look, gran was gone.

The next morning Jim let his daughter out in front of the mortuary. She went into the business office, off the beautiful large living room of the mortuary. Amber took gran's outfit and bag of accessories from Mandy and gave them to the funeral staff. Amber chatted with her for a few minutes. Mandy began to feel positive about the celebration. Amber made her feel so at home, like talking with an older sister.

"Would you like to walk with me to the reception area, where your grandmother's family and friends will celebrate her life?"

"Yes, I need to walk, to stay active; it helps with my sadness."

They went over the layout of the reception room, where the caterers needed to set up the finger food, cake, coffee, and Christmas punch, a little cranberry but a mostly strawberry punch.

Mandy counted out the round tables, and chairs, 12 tables and six chairs at each table.

"Oh Amber, this looks great. I think folks will come kinda in waves, maybe the students and their parents first, then friends later."

"Right, St. Paul's is just a few blocks away."

Amber walked with her out to the large entrance living room of the mortuary.

"Would you mind if I sit here for a little while?"

"Go right ahead."

Amber pointed out the remembrance Christmas tree placed near the middle of the room.

"Ah, this is the tree you were telling me about."

"Every Christmas, we have a short ceremony on a Sunday afternoon near Christmas, for families we helped. They come to remember their loved ones. I know of several couples who've attended for the last 15 years; folks who lost children, and other family members."

"That's just so awesome, a really special way to remember someone."

"It's very popular, part of the holiday celebration for families. I'll leave you for a few minutes while I call the caterers with final instructions. You know they will also do the serving and cleanup."

"Right, as my parents and I decided."

Mandy sat on the comfortable couch, with a view of the towering tree. She closed her eyes and rested. The sound of running water caught her attention. She got up and moved to a stone wall, from which water flowed continually. In niches of the stone she found smooth rocks with wording on them. Mandy reached out to one rock at arm's length.   She didn't touch it but burst into tears. She sat down hard on the small seating area in front of the wall.

Amber found Mandy gripping the seat with her hands. Tears poured down her face. Amber sat down next to Mandy and held her shoulder. They sat together until Mandy quieted. Amber handed her several tissues which she used to mop her face.

"It's finally hit me, what's happened to gran."

"Which stone, which words?"

"Yeah, the one about, though we held you in our arms for awhile, we hold you in our hearts forever."

"Says it all."

"Oh, Amber," Mandy moved a little away from her, "thank you for being here right now, for helping me with the reception. I want it to be fun, especially for the little ones, her students. Will you be there, for the reception?"

"I will be, your gran's funeral, all parts of it, are under my control."

"Then you know about that we won't be at the grave after the reception. You folks will take care of everything, you know, bury gran. We'll want to visit the gravesite at Landview Cemetery, probably Christmas Day, and then again, when the gravestone is placed. Uh, you're doing that, the gravestone?"

"Exactly, your dad gave me permission to move ahead with the stone, minimal instructions, just name, year of birth and death."

"I figured the minimal part. Dad, his assessor job, this time of year, the property taxes thing. Sorry, he's just got too much going on. Anyway, is it possible for me to add four words, at the bottom of the gravestone?"

"Certainly."

Mandy pulled a half sheet of paper from her coat pocket and handed it to Amber.

"She served with love," Amber read out loud, her own voice cracking.

Mandy began to cry again, and Amber held her in a hug for a little while, rocking her side to side.

"I have to go, and I know you have a big job to do. I really had no idea how involved the death process is. Thank you again for being so gracious to me. I have a good feeling about gran's celebration."

"So we'll see you tomorrow."

"Oh my gosh, that's right, tomorrow's gran's big day."

Amber watched Mandy smile to her and squeezed her hand. Mandy waved to her as she left the mortuary.

ℰℴ

"I'm so sorry, Mandy."

Mandy and Sally Ann hugged after Mandy let her in the Overton home.

"What can I do, to help you?"

Sally Ann began to sob and Mandy joined in. They held on tight to each other for several minutes. After they let go, Mandy found tissues, and they mopped their faces and noses.

"How long can you stay?"

"Mom will pick me up after she gets off work, three hours."

"So, Michael's due home soon. He had to help out at the detachment; why he wasn't here before today. His job is to decorate our Christmas tree. Mine is to bring up the ornaments and the tree stand. Mom and dad wanted to skip this holiday completely. I held my ground and insisted us kids deserved the special holiday. Dad and I got a tree last night, starting to dry out, but it was cheap. Most everybody's already got their tree."

"Hey, gran wants you to still have Christmas."

"Right, Sally Ann, she's here with us."

"I know, girl, can't see her, but I feel her presence."

Through the years Sally Ann often came home from school with Mandy and Mary Beth. Her mom would pick her up about the same time one of Mandy's parents stopped by.

"I love gran; I don't know my own grandmothers very well, but she's the best," Sally Ann said as she smiled to

Mandy. "And I was so super lucky, gran, Mrs. Overton, was my third grade teacher, and she positively rocked as a teacher."

"Yeah, I couldn't be her student; she made that very clear. So I had the other third grade teacher. But I made the best of the situation; gran insisted on that."

"And gran took us to Girl Scouts, through those years, Daisy, then Brownie, then for a little while, the Girl Scouts. She used to talk to us about the 3 C's, courage, confidence, and character."

Sally Ann smiled to Mandy, "You really've become a model of a scout; it's gonna carry you on as you grow."

"Same for you, Sally Ann, a model of character. Are we ready to do this Christmas stuff?"

She nodded to Mandy as they walked to the back porch.

"It's kinda heavy, let's take our time."

Mandy helped Sally Ann wrap a large piece of plastic around the tree before they carried it in slow fashion from the back porch through the open kitchen to the large great room. They unwrapped the tree after they set it against the wall, in the area where the tree always got placed.

"Uh, the tree, it doesn't look so bad."

They swept up the needles from around the tree. Then they brought up the box of ornaments and lights and the tree stand.

"Thanks, that's such a help. Let's get us some hot chocolate and sugar cookies. Mom's been super unsettled; she's shared about her regrets in not getting along with gran. Now she realizes it's pretty late, to make any kind of amends."

They sat together, blowing the steam from their cups, sipping the hot chocolate, and eating cookies.

"Shouldn't say anything, Mandy, but you know me."

"Yeah, I know you, you'll speak your mind, just like I often do."

"Right, it's too bad, but now your mom's gotta live with those regrets. It could'a gone so much better for your mom and gran."

Sally Ann watched Mandy nod, her eyes clouded and her lips set in a severe straight line. After they cleaned up at the kitchen island, they headed to Mandy's room. She looked around, a light lavender, very calming room, with a small wooden desk and a small wooden bookcase filled with her favorite books. Her windows, one on the east and one on the south, they brought in wonderful light, the special part of her room. Sally Ann sat on Mandy's twin bed, with its white bedspread and red pillows.

"Gran and I, well, my Christmas present this year, I got it early. She asked me what I wanted. And I told her I wanted a different look for myself. We went and got the tangled mess of my hair cut, to a shorter, more manageable length. And I'm using a curling iron on the ends, to give it a little curl. Do you like it?"

"Yeah, really I do. Mandy, you're beautiful, but all that hair in your face, couldn't really see you."

"So, that was part of it, and then, I gotta show you."

Mandy went to her closet and laid out seven new winter outfits, skirts, some pleated and some flared, above the knees, turtlenecks and sweaters to mix and match, and tights in several different colors to match the outfits.

"And my boots, my favorite part, I can wear them out in the snow, and also inside."

"Mandy, your new clothes, I like your stuff for school. What about for spring and summer?"

"Gran said she already bought that stuff, and it's sitting in her closet. She planned on giving me the clothes this spring, after the snows, when the trees blossom."

"So, you'll get to see that stuff when you clear her closet."

"Right."

"Your folks're overwhelmed."

"That's for sure; mom's just absolutely quiet, dad's taking the lead."

"Mandy."

"Yeah?"

"I can pick you up for church on Sundays, uh my folks and me; I'd like to do that. Gran took you, well, before now. God's with us, always, Mandy. I'm sure you think He's forgotten, how could He do this to you, and with Christ's birth coming?"

"Pretty angry at God right now, know it'll get better. Gran will help me with that. Sally Ann, you may not believe it, gran appeared to me, after I left her home, when I carried the outfit and stuff the mortuary would need to dress her."

"Wow, that's so special, Mandy. And she talked to you?"

"Yeah, she walked right beside me on my way home. She looked so pretty with her blonde hair curled the way she does it, and in her blue long winter coat."

"Oh my goodness, oh Mandy," Sally looked into her bright brown eyes.

"Uh huh," Mandy nodded.

Sally watched Mandy's smiling eyes.

℘

"Oh gran, this is so much fun. I'm sure you're watching us."

Every third grade parent or family member brought their child to Mrs. Overton's celebration at the mortuary after the short church funeral service.   As Mandy predicted, the children enjoyed the snacks, cake, and punch.   After they ate, they gathered around Mandy's folks.

Daniel got appointed spokesman for the group.

"We love Mrs. Overton," he nodded his head emphatically. "And we want to remember her, so here's what we want to do."

He handed the envelope to Jim Overton. He read the card, then stood and looked over the gathering. He smiled to the children standing around him.

"I see a large number of signatures on this card. This coming spring mom's class will plant a tree in the school yard, a tree to honor Mrs. Mary Beth Overton."

Jim started clapping, the children began clapping, and soon the whole group stood, clapping and cheering. He sat down, the tears streaming from his eyes, at the gesture from the young people. When it quieted Jim Overton heard a small voice.

"Don't cry, Mr. Overton, please sing with us, sing Christmas carols for Mrs. Overton," a small third grade student pleaded with him.

And so they proceeded, the children stood near the family, and they all sang carols, ending with "Silent Night."

"Oh, there's one more."

They all broke into song, the students moving throughout the crowd, singing "We Wish You a Merry Christmas."

ℬ

Michael drove Mandy home from the celebration.

"Sis, that's awesome, the whole celebration, the folks, they said you pretty much handled the whole service and reception."

"Right, Michael, they're super in shock, and totally bumbed out about everything."

"It really hasn't hit me yet, even though I saw grandma in the casket. Wow, is she ever a beautiful lady."

"You'd never noticed that before?"

"She's my grandma, and no, I guess I never did notice."

"Granddad Overton didn't show up; neither did Uncle Justin, her own son. Unbelievable, how much really tough stuff's gone on in our family. But, hey Michael, I did call granddad and asked him to contact Uncle Justin. Gosh, he even thanked me for the call."

"That's for sure, really tough stuff; after their divorce seven years ago, gran and granddad, just no communication, ever between each other, same with Uncle Justin, gran, and dad. I can't even imagine what terrible stuff happened to make them so alienated." He paused, "Mandy, I'm sure it's for the best."

"And mom, her never getting along with gran, that put a strain on everything."

"Right, are you and mom, you know," he paused, "is it better for the two of you?"

"It is; I've done a lot of growing up, shook off a lot of the crap from the past. And I've let go of that awful jealousy I always had for you. My big brother, the super star, smart, handsome, athletic, a bright personality. I was always a disappointment to the folks, not as smart, or attractive, like you are. They even called me weird a few times, my taste in books, things I liked to eat, even my appearance sometimes, lots of conflict, good grief," Mandy turned and shook her head to her brother.

Michael and Mandy parked in front of their home, leaving room for their parents to park their cars in the garage. Both parents had to go back to work. They had last minute items to finish before the holiday.

"Hey, today, at the funeral, and later at the reception, you looked very nice. You need to know that." He touched her shoulder, "Mandy, you're becoming a beautiful young lady. Dude, you'll be getting a car, before too long."

"Yeah, Michael, I can't wait."

"Still babysitting?"

"Uh huh, I got a New Year's Eve gig, gonna spend the night so the parents can rock out at a hotel celebration. I'll come home New Year's Day. But I plan to get a real job starting next summer."

"You're super ambitious."

"Thanks, I got a mighty fine big brother to thank for that, your example."

"You used to not think I was so OK."

"Uh huh, but I was a brat, and just didn't get it. Now I see, in three and a half years you'll commission as a second lieutenant in the U.S. Air Force."

"And?"

"Oh yeah, and graduate with a degree in chemistry; you'll be a military officer lab rat."

"Right, I can't wait for the research we'll do, unbelievable stuff going on in military research."

"Let's head in."

Before Mandy put her key in the front door, her brother turned her to him and gave her a hug.

"I hadn't had the chance to do that; I know you're sad, missing gran, you really were closer to her than you were to mom. It's up to us, Sis, to make this holiday work, to help mom and dad with all the stuff involved in a death. We can do this, right?"

"Right," she nodded to him and tried to smile.

℘

Mandy helped Michael decorate the tree. They sang Christmas carols and slid their presents to each other and their folks under the tree.

"Not sure when, for the presents," Mandy touched her brother's arm.

He saw the tears in her eyes, "I'll make sure it happens, Sis."

"Nice," Cindy commented when she saw the lighted tree. "You two decided to go with colored lights this year."

"Yeah, bright and cheerful, with all our ornaments, from our small kid days," Michael added.

Mandy fixed a family holiday favorite for Christmas Eve, tomato soup, and toasted cheese sandwiches. She set the table with festive Christmas place mats and holiday paper napkins. Michael helped her with the toasted cheese sandwiches.

"Remember, I got a big appetite," he reminded her, "so I know I can eat three sandwiches, best if we microwave them, OK?"

"That's good, thanks."

The family sat together at the dining room table, holding hands. Together they said a grace from Emerson, "'Be thankful, for each new morning with its light, for rest and shelter of the night, for health and food, for love and friends, for everything Thy goodness sends.'"

They kept the conversation light, discussing Michael's next semester and his classes, and Mandy's babysitting, and her great grades for the just completed semester of her freshman year.

She thought to herself at the end of dinner, "Wow, they didn't discuss Michael's grades; I'm sure he did OK."

Before they got up from the table Cindy touched Mandy's hand, smiled to her and then spoke out to them all, "We are very grateful, Mandy, for the way you handled both the church memorial, and the grand reception. You are so grown up; I can hardly believe it was you speaking from your heart, in front of all the folks gathered at church for Mary Beth, thank you."

Mandy watched her dad nod to her, his teary eyes and his emphatic smile.

Michael whispered, "God bless us all."

Michael and Mandy decided to attend the midnight candlelight service at St. Paul's. The parents wanted to relax and head to bed early. They all agreed they would go to Mary Beth's gravesite the next morning, after opening presents, and Christmas breakfast. When he first got to town, Michael picked up a ham and a pumpkin pie he and Mandy would fix for Christmas dinner.

ഹ

Owen gazed ahead as the midnight candlelight service proceeded.

"This is such a time of joy," he thought as he looked to his left and to his right. His whole family sat together here, at church, his mom and dad, brother, Matthew, home from college and his memaw.

With his tall frame he saw over most everyone's heads.

"She's there, dark blonde, and with her brother, him in a blue uniform, sitting two rows ahead and to the right side. She's on our cross country team, and fast, scary fast, Mandy.

And I feel sad for her, losing her grandma, Mrs. Overton. Mrs. Overton was my third grade teacher, sweet, tough, hard on us, but fair. We all sure loved her, back in the day when we were little and loved our teachers, our day-time moms," he nodded as he remembered her.

After the service Owen made certain he found Mandy and her brother, walking down the church steps to the sidewalk.

"Mandy," he stopped them.

"Owen," she looked up and smiled, "wasn't it a nice service?"

"For sure," he looked at Michael. "I'm Owen; Mandy and I were on the cross country team."

Owen extended his hand to Michael.

"Owen, I graduated about the time you two got to high school."

"But I still got to see you play football and basketball, what an athlete."

"Thanks," he nodded and smiled to them both, "it was a lot of fun."

Owen turned to Mandy, "I'm so sorry about your grandma."

"Yeah, the whole family's just numb. We're taking it just a day at a time."

"Yeah, Owen, I'll be able to be here for a week, before I head back to school. So I'm going to help out with a lot of stuff; Mandy and I've already assigned ourselves tasks to take care of, on grandma's behalf. Mom and dad, they gotta work, can't take a lot of time off."

"You two take good care of yourselves; God bless and keep you and your family. And I hope you can take a little time to try to enjoy this holiday."

Mandy and Michael nodded to him and watched Owen return to his family. They headed home very early on this Christmas Day.

⁊

"We've gotten so much done, Mandy."

They stood in gran's great room.

"Yeah, meeting the realtor in a few minutes. I'm so glad you called her to get instructions about how to prepare gran's home for sale. She wants the look to be minimal, just a bit of furniture, no clutter, no personal pictures, or weird eccentricities."

Michael nodded to his sister as he started to see her smile.

"She sure helped us, giving us the names of the junk service, the nonprofits, and the mover company she uses for situations like ours. It worked out great; we could'a never done this without their help."

"Right, Sis, you'll remember to ask the realtor about her hiring a snow removal person to take care of gran's sidewalks and driveway while the house is up for sale."

"Oh yeah, it's on my list; oh Michael," she paused and shook her head to her brother. "I think the house's gonna be hard to sell, dead of winter, and, oh my gosh, the whole economy, some serious stuff's gonna happen before long. The good news so far is that home mortgages are pretty easy to get now. I'm so glad you'll have a job when you graduate."

"So you think jobs'll be affected?"

"Yeah, big time, dad and mom; I think, are gonna have to tighten up their departments, mom especially, in the country clerk's office. I can really see that she'll maybe lose an employee or two."

"You're talking about it at school?"

"Yup, affecting, or gonna affect most every aspect of our lives, our families, us kids, for sure."

"You must think about what you want to do, Mandy."

"Yeah, I'm already doing that; mom and dad say they saved for my college. We'll see about that."

"Let's walk through the house; that'll for sure bring the realtor."

Over the past week a great deal of gran's furniture and possessions got listed and donated to a nonprofit. That was after Michael and Mandy went through the house with their parents, finding out what they might want as a remembrance of Mary Beth. The parents and children asked for only a very few items which already got transported to the Overton basement.

Mrs. Dominic arrived and did a rapid look through the entire home.

"It's ready to show; clean, decluttered, personal stuff gone. Whoever's interested, I'm certain, will want an inspector to check out the entire home, inside and out. The roof, with the snow, that'll have to wait to be looked over, that is, if I can find your family a buyer."

"One good thing is that the home is paid for; gran made certain of that. I know our folks are ready for it to be on the market for as long as it takes."

"Of course, you'll keep the electricity and gas on," Mrs. Dominic nodded to them."And so it doesn't look like no one lives here."

"Yeah, I've already rigged a timer to a lamp in the living room, goes on at 5 p.m. and off at 7 a.m."

"And the family'll stop by to make sure the lamp light bulb doesn't burn out."

"Good."

"Mom and dad are taking us out to dinner, for all we did to help out," Mandy said as they let themselves out of gran's home.

ℰↄ

"Heading back to Ames tomorrow?"

"First thing, stuff to do at the detachment, and getting my dorm room in order."

The Overton family sat together at a favorite Italian restaurant on the outskirts of Porttown. After they ordered, Jim Overton looked around at his family. He smiled to Mandy and Michael.

"Your mom and I went through the reading of grandma's will with her lawyer this morning. There were a few details, but to let you know, she left $20,000 to each of you, for your expenses in the future. That, of course is for your college educations. We'll add that to the money we've saved for college. And Mandy, grandma's car is yours, if you want it; it'll be some months before you can start driving with one of us with you."

"Uh, what about Michael, a car?"

"Honey," Cindy touched Mandy's shoulder, "we bought a car for Michael."

"So, Sis, I'm covered. I love my wheels to pieces, so great in the snow."

"Oh my gosh, gran, she did super good driving in snow too. I can't believe it; the car is?"

"Five years old and paid for, so it, hopefully, 'll last you through high school and college. It's a nice looking sedan."

Mandy smiled, "Wow, it is; I for sure'll get a job as soon as I can, to pay for gas and insurance."

"We'll help you with part of your insurance, like we help Michael."

"So Mandy, after work tomorrow, mom and I will come home, take a car and get grandma's car out of her garage. That way the garage will be completely clear; no evidence of who lived there before the house went up for sale."

"Yeah, depersonalize the property."

"Right, Michael."

Mandy watched her dad nod to them.

"So, guys, where will the car be parked?"

"There's room to the left of the garage; that's where it'll have to sit until you can drive it, Mandy."

"That'll be hard on it."

"Your mom and I will drive it once in a while; we'll keep it insured and with up-to-date license plates. Then when you start driving we'll transfer title and get the car in your name, just like we did with Michael's."

"Mom and dad, that'll be expensive."

Cindy smiled to her daughter, "Thank you for thinking about the expense, Mandy. But that's not so bad; we at least don't have to buy a car."

Michael looked at his family, "You all've really started to work everything out. I thought I'd be super worried about you all when I left for school. But it looks like things, well," he nodded.

"Yeah, the brain fog, losing her, the shock is fading a tiny bit," Jim paused. "That's because of you two, helping us so much, this last week, and Mandy, everything connected with grandma's death. And Christmas, it felt special to have peace and quiet in our home, opening our presents, the fire, singing Christmas carols at grandma's grave. We even laughed while we played games."

"Yum, chow's here."

"We're all starved!" exclaimed Cindy.

That night before bed Mandy opened her bottom desk drawer, where she kept treasures from her life. She took out a packet of blue envelopes, from the very bottom of the drawer. They were addressed to Mary Beth, written in her granddad's bold pen and tied together with a bright red ribbon.

Mandy found them, under her grandma's pretty panties, slips, and hankies, in a drawer that she cleared as she and Michael got gran's home ready for sale. That empty chest of drawers, along with a lot of other furniture, got designated for pick up to a nonprofit.

"These are important, right gran? I'll keep the letters safe; I'm not ready to share these with anyone."

Mandy sat at her desk, patted the envelopes as the lump in her throat enlarged. She felt hot tears scouring her eyes.

"You never spoke about it, gran, but whatever happened between you and granddad, oh my gosh, so much sadness, granddad leaving town so fast."

Mandy put her head down on the desk. Then she heard the whisper.

"You aren't ready to read these yet; I'll let you know when."

"Gran, you're here," Mandy lifted her head and smiled through her tears.

"I love you, Mandy."

Mandy waited for her gran to continue talking to her. But she heard only silence.

"She's gone away again. Such a surprise, to hear her voice, I gotta remember what she said, about the letters."

That made her think about the special treatment the mortuary gave the Overton family. Mandy found a thank you note and wrote a quick note to Amanda.

Amanda, and all the staff,

The Overton family sends a special thanks for all you've done for us, and for Mary Beth. We'll not forget your caring and concern for our family.

Sincerely, Mandy and all the Overton Family

2

Junior Year – 2008

Late that summer she submitted her resume to Hotchkisson Mortuary. Mandy created the resume as she learned in her business class. To go with the resume she had a reference letter from the family for whom she babysat for the past three years. The children were 1, 3, and 5 when Mandy started caring for them.

She watched them grow in big spurts, now 4, 7, and 9 year-olds. That reference letter became the key to her interview with the mortuary. She knew how to manage.

"That's just a terrible idea; why in the name of heaven would you want to work in a mortuary?"

Her dad could hardly keep from shouting at her as they sat down to dinner. Mandy winced as his cutting tone shook her.

"Mandy, why not just get a job in a store?" her mom pleaded.

"Mom, Dad," she took a deep breath and let it out, "I pretty much have made up my mind. I want to go to mortuary school; I want to become a mortician."

"That's the most morbid, unbelievably cracked-brain idea I ever heard of, Mandy."

She heard her dad's anger as he practically spat the words out. She looked over and gave her dad eye contact.

"I accepted the job; I'll help out in the office Mondays, Wednesdays, and Fridays after school until mortuary close, usually at 5. I'll have some Saturdays and Sundays working also."

ℰ

Mandy came back to the present, blowing out a big sigh as she left school for the walk to work. She felt a little weary, this Friday before Thanksgiving break.

"And gran, I did it. I didn't let my folks get to me. Remember you told me to never back down from who I am and what I want to be. I'm coping. My folks gave me more chores, like I swear, to spite me. I'm handling everything, plus making good grades."

"Mandy, Mandy."

She heard the voice and turned to see Owen walking to her. They were a block away from school.

He caught up with her and smiled, "Mandy, I wanna go out with you."

"Owen, gosh, I'd like that, but what about cross country?"

He watched her eyes widen.

"Ah, season's almost over, all the practices and meets. You always headed out right after school. I missed that you weren't on the team this fall, missed your smile," he paused, "and you."

"Work, I've a job after school, a job that I like so much, serving folks when they're at their absolute lowest, depths of despair."

She turned and smiled up to him, looking into his dark eyes.

"Yeah, meet somewhere, uh, during the break?"

"Sounds nice, I've got a life celebration to help set up. And I work Thanksgiving week, Friday, a full day, and Monday and Wednesday, afternoons; what about next Saturday afternoon?"

"I'll figure it out with my family. We're still prepping the ground for the next corn crop."

"Call me; it'd be fun to catch up; we don't have any classes together."

He touched her hand, "I wish you and your family a happy Thanksgiving."

"Gosh, thanks, and to your family," she nodded to him.

"I'm happy; I've wanted to be with her for a long time," Owen whispered as he ran the block back to school and the student parking lot to pick up his car.

Mandy hurried along to the mortuary. She felt a fierce shock smack her, like she'd run into a door.

"Owen, he wants to go out with," she paused, "me. Girls really want to be with him; sheesh, I see them with him, hotties." She stopped for a second, shook her head, and spoke out, "Wonder what he sees in me?"

The thought left her as she walked with quick steps into the mortuary. She helped with the printing of the small pamphlets the mortuary created for the family of a deceased person. Amber asked for her assistance in the reception area, even though it was a week early. They set the reception up according to the family's instructions. For this affair the family ordered and paid for pizza to be delivered. The family would furnish several kinds of beverages. The mortuary did not have a liquor license, so no alcohol could be served.

Mandy left at 5 p.m. for the trek home. As she walked along, she watched the sunlight give way to evening shadows. It gave her a chance to think about the life celebration next Friday morning. It involved a 19-year-old community college student. The young man overdosed on some pretty bad heroin.

She let herself in and changed from her school/work clothes into comfortable blue jeans and the ISU sweatshirt Michael gave her last Christmas.

"God," she knelt by her bed, "You know I can't talk to my folks much about what I do; they're just so opposed to my whole deal. But God, help me to keep from being insensitive to the suffering I'm gonna see. This is my third OD funeral since I started in the summer. You are in charge, Your will, I guess these OD'd people just thought they'd live forever, nothin' could touch them. Hah, You and I know better. God, guide me in being helpful, polite, to acknowledge the agony this family feels. Amber is my mentor; I must follow her lead."

Mandy hopped up and headed downstairs to start the pizza. And she heard from Owen.

"Next Saturday afternoon, let's meet at the diner downtown."

"Sweet," she paused, "2 p.m., and Owen, Happy Thanksgiving to you and your family."

"And to you and your folks, also."

The Grenson grandparents drove in from Ohio for the Thanksgiving time. Mandy pitched in wherever she was needed in helping with Thanksgiving dinner.

"We'll do it my way," Mary Grenson smiled as she looked to her daughter, Cindy, and granddaughter, Mandy.

Mandy began to giggle, "Oh Grandma Grenson, or the highway."

The three women laughed. And Mandy knew, from the other times she was with this grandmother that Mary, indeed, was in charge. She also remembered several terrible verbal fights between Mary and Mandy's other grandmother, gran. Both women were Type A, very knowing, assertive types.

Mandy saw that her mom, Cindy, continued to be cheerful during the time that her parents visited. It was super calmer, when Mary Beth Overton was not present in the family.

After her grandparents and parents went to bed that evening, Mandy sat in front of the dying fire. She shook her head, "All the chaos this family used to have between the adults, it's kinda gone away. I'm happy."

Mandy got up early the next morning and made a big pot of coffee for her parents, grandparents and brother. She sipped a small cup of coffee and had a cinnamon roll. She remembered; there would be lots of coffee for the staff at the mortuary.

The staff warned her. Mandy never witnessed such wretched heartbreak. The teen's mother remained inconsolable. The family doctor gave her a sedative before the gathering at the mortuary. She was held up by her two brothers, as she moved about. The father kept quiet, throughout the gathering. Mandy sort of knew the story. The boy went to rehab twice, but each time he relapsed.

"Third time," Mandy shook her head, "he went to God."

The mood lightened after the brief service as food brought folks together in the reception area. An older brother and sister of the teen came home from their colleges for the ceremony. They had to go back for finals coming up. The smell of pizza and chocolate cupcakes wafted past Mandy's nose as she helped keep glasses filled with pop and water, and cups filled with coffee or tea for all the guests.

After the third time that the teen's mother broke down during the reception, two family members took her away. Mandy finally had a chance to ask Amber, the in-charge person for this funeral, what was going on with this family.

Amber pulled her away from the group to a corner of the kitchen area and whispered to her.

"The mother's been in rehab herself; they released her for the funeral, but she's gotta head back."

"Where's God?" Amber watched Mandy tear up as she asked.

Amber touched her shoulder, "With us, always, He has His plan for each of us."

"I guess I need to get used to this, the OD's, the suicides."

"Yes, these situations are a part of living. Remember, one of our jobs is to help ease the pain, of those struggling."

"Thanks, Amber, it's the timing of this one, the day after Thanksgiving, a time when most folks express gratitude. Gosh, maybe, God will help this mom get better."

"At least, my prayer, and my hope."

જી

Owen rose from the table and gave Mandy a hug as she met him in the little café. He chose a table for two in a corner, where they could talk in private, away from the chatter of others.

They shared about their Thanksgiving dinners. Each of them had a brother come home from college to join in the delicious chow.

"Why do they call you "mortuary girl" at school, Mandy?"

She eyed him from across the small table and giggled.

"Hey, it's partly a mocking, making fun, a little jealousy. I simply state that I'm mortuary girl. So you need to know that I'm learning everything I can about helping the dead, their families as they come to us. Like all the mortuary staff, I have a deep faith in God. We'll all go to Him one day. We attempt to ease pain in survivors, often times the shock of losing someone, like unexpectedly. Folks are often in terrible emotional distress when they come to us. They really need help."

"Wow, I had no idea, only going to one funeral, of my papow, a grandparent I did get to spend some time with, when I was younger."

"Yeah, Owen, that's what I do. My parents hate my whole working thing. They think I'm crackbrained (dad's word) to be doing this work. It is my calling. It's what I will study when I leave Porttown High."

He gazed into her eyes, "You impress me so much. You know what you want and from what I've just heard, you know how to go about getting it. To compliment you is one thing I've wanted to do for a long time. You always dress nice for school, always with a skirt and top and tights to match. It makes you super distinctive looking. Now I know why, 'cause you go to work in an office when you leave school. And it's not just an ordinary office."

"Right, it certainly isn't. Often clients are there when I arrive from school. That quiet and polite image we all portray is really crucial. One day I want to take over a mortuary."

"Whoah, Mandy, that's a super big deal goal, running a business like that."

"Uh huh."

"So, it's mortician school, what you want to do?"

"Yup, Mortuary Science, need an AA, that's lots of general classes, and then the 50 or so credits in Mortuary Science, plus an internship, it's critical."

"Dude, that's like a college degree."

She watched Owen's eyes widen as he began to realize what would be ahead for her in the next few years.

"Yeah, very specialized."

They talked about cross country and Mandy admitted that she missed being with the team, and the running. She shared with Owen that she started running on her own on weekends, the being outside a natural high.

"I've told you a bit about me, now it's your turn. You run so fast, but," she paused, "who are you, Owen?" she asked as her brown eyes shown into his dark brown eyes.

"Farmer's son, I love God, and He loves me. So I know corn, been around it all my life. My brother, Matt, he's at University of Iowa. And he says flat out he wants nuthin' to do with the farm. So dad's turning it over to me, a little at a time. My folks want me to take some business classes, get my AA, maybe agribusiness, and Mandy," he stopped and looked up and ahead for a moment, "the situation in the Middle East."

"Ooohhh, we've lost several of our own from around here, the last three years."

She shook her head, and he watched a shadow cast over the brown in her eyes.

"Yeah, well I've just about made up my mind; I'm going Air Force National Guard, as soon as I graduate. I want to help my country, just maybe not active duty. When I'm done with that, I'll get to a community college to take classes, have the college experience. I'm gonna try to do a lot of that and still help get the corn crops in."

"Uh, that's Octobers?"

Owen watched her eyebrows rise in questioning.

"That's right," he nodded.

"Uh, do you think it's kinda unusual, to know what we want to do, at our age?"

"Maybe, but for sure, you, you certainly have your plan."

"Yeah, far as I can, think it's God's plan for me."

He looked into her eyes, "Still can't figure, where'd the mortuary desire come from?"

"My gran, Mrs. Overton, your third grade teacher; when she died, a special lady at the mortuary helped me so much, understood what I was going through, spent time with me, stuff my parents weren't equipped to do, the shock of gran's death."

"So you'll help others suffering with loss, like you've been helped."

"Exactly."

"Mandy, you have a calling."

"So will you have, Owen, serving your country, in the guard."

"What about your friends?"

"The couple I have, think I'm ambitious, still kinda weird, and I suspect they have some jealousy, in knowing what I want. Yeah, we won't be floundering around for years, trying to figure out what we want to do."

"For sure, one day, business people, Mandy, you didn't know me the last couple of years, 'cept cross country."

"I do remember a messed up leg somewhere in there. I saw you once in a while, swinging along on your crutches."

They drank some of their refilled cups of coffee.

"Yeah, but I gotta." He stopped and started to tear up. "Uh, gotta let you know what happened as the leg healed."

"OK?" she questioned and saw tears glistening in his eyes.

"Last summer I had to go to rehab."

She looked at him with bright expectant eyes.

"What the heck happened?"

"Narcotic I got prescribed for my leg pain, I got addicted, in just a few days."

"One of those, whose body."

He cut in, "That's right, one of those, except you see the dead body."

"And you got cleaned up, in rehab?" she gave him a sharp look.

Owen watched her lips thin, and her eyes turn a piercing dark brown as she said, "That you'll have to watch yourself all the days of your life."

"Whew," he put his hand to his head for a moment. He nodded to her, "You've already seen so much, at the mortuary, the end result of addiction. Yeah, I'll have to watch myself every day, like you say, for the rest of my life."

She let out a big breath, "That took enormous courage, guts, to share that with me, Owen, and I'm so sorry that happened to you."

Mandy nodded to him and gave him a small smile.

"It's important that you know."

"And you need to know that even the smell of alcohol makes me sick; that's another thing that's happened, working where I do.'

"The stench, pretty bad, when the corpse first comes in?"

"Yeah, like the body took a bath in the stuff." She paused and nodded, "You do understand."

"Pretty grim conversation, Mandy, I got a lot better picture of you now, a caring person who's learning to take death in stride."

"Absolutely, and as gran said 'it'll be tough sledding for me', like my folks opposing what I want to do. But I will go forward in my training. And God, He's the knowing One; He alone knows how long each of us has to do our work."

Owen touched her hand with his own.

"Oh my, each day is so precious."

"Right; I gotta head over to the library. Mom will pick me up there; she had to go in today. But in just a few days, I'll have my license."

She smiled broadly to him, and he watched her brown eyes dance with happiness."

"Wheels?"

"Yea, gran's."

"LLLuuuuccckkkyyy," he drawled out the word.

They laughed together.

"Yeah, and mom and dad're helping me with insurance. They've kept the car up since gran died, licensed, and insured."

"But you gotta help some."

She nodded, "This's been fun, to get to know you better. We ran together in cross country, but not much chance to talk personal."

"I want to see you again, Mandy."

"And I want to see you."

ℰℴ

The week before Christmas Owen invited Mandy to the Sunday noon meal after church. She drove to the Northwood farm, two miles outside town. She knew Sara and Brad from running cross country. She remembered that one or the other parent came to every meet in which Owen ran. The year before, Mandy came in, usually, second or third, among the women who ran in the meets. She liked the applause, but she loved the high, like riding above the ground without her feet even touching. She felt that as she bounded along on whatever trail the runners took. Now, because of her work, she had to give up cross country. She missed it, but found a running trail she used on Sunday afternoons.

Owen took her to the kitchen after they greeted each other and he hung up her coat. She nodded and said hello to his parents and shook Brad's hand.

Brad spoke in a gravelly low voice, "Sure miss your wide smile and speedy running at the meets we go to now."

Mandy held the plate of chocolate chip bars in one hand. She handed them to Sara after she shook hands with her.

She made eye contact with each parent and smiled, "Yeah, I miss the running, but I work."

Owen gazed at her, a tall and slender girl, with a smile that lit up her whole world.

"I wanted to bring something; I know you folks work hard, just like mine do."

"Thanks, Mandy, real thoughtful," Sara nodded to her.

They held hands for grace. Owen did the honors and at the end of grace he thanked God that Mandy could join them.

"Everything's delicious, Sara, I do most of the cooking at my home. It's so nice to eat someone else's great food."

Mandy spoke that out to Sara as the three of them cleared the table. They joined Brad for dessert and coffee at the couches. They sat in a semicircle around a warm and cozy wood stove placed on one side of the living room.

"Uuummm, the cherry pie, what do you do, almond flavoring?"

Mandy turned to Sara for an answer, "Right, plus more sugar. Otherwise the cherries taste blah, flat."

"We want to know you, Mandy."

"What's Owen shared?"

"Not that much; we want to hear from you. It's certainly clear to us that you work with lots of adults, and have a self-assurance we don't see in young ladies of your age. You're not a bit intimidated about meeting parents of a boy you're seeing."

"Thanks, Brad," Mandy paused and giggled, "yeah, I'm used to adults, folks in terrible emotional pain. I'd like to think of myself as an angel among those folks, just like firemen, EMT's, police, medical staff, all angels."

"Goodness, Mandy, so well said," Sara nodded to her.

"My folks, they've been really upset about what I do. I think it's fear, like we all have, dying, and everything that goes with it. For me, going to God at death, it's ultimate joy, really going Home. Still, my parents, they say they'll help me with the money for college. To let you know, they really don't have to, 'cause my gran gave my brother and me money designated specifically for school. At least I'll have that."

"So, what will school be like for you?" Brad asked.

"AA with more business classes as electives, then mortuary science, 50 plus hours, and I'll do an internship. It'll end up being over three years. I'll be able to get my AA and the mortuary science all at the same community college campus. Then there's national exams, state accreditation, like with most fields, to determine competency."

"Mandy, tell them your plan after that," Owen spoke up.

"Right," she paused and looked around at them, "I want to return to Porttown, to work in the mortuary I'm helping in now. Mr. Hotchkisson, he's thinking ahead to retirement in six or so years. And I've talked to him. I'd like to buy half the business at that time; then one day, buy him out, and take over the business. It thrives."

"So you want to return to Porttown."

"Yes, I want to do an internship in another mortuary setting, another town. But Porttown, it's a solid community, with lots of good people, in town, and you folks, our farmers, really our future."

"My goodness, Mandy, that's quite a plan," Sara smiled to her.

"My plan, but God's helping me think it all out, His plan, also."

"And so you know, Owen's talked to you about his future?"

"He has; he wants to serve his country, and," Mandy nodded and gave Owen eye contact, "he cares fiercely for this land, your land, in your family and what they've done now for the generations the Northwood family's lived here."

≪⌒

Mandy drove home on the snowpacked road.

"I'm so happy I got to help Amber," she nodded. "It was a reception, sheesh, so much like gran's two years ago."

She thought back to that Christmas time two years ago for a moment, a Christmas that ended with peace. Once again, she realized why. Her gran was out of the picture, and that made Mandy's mom more settled. Her grandma and her daughter always had a strained relationship.

"Gran's reception, I'll always remember that," she smiled as she parked in front of her home.

Once inside she put on her pleasant at-home face and her just-get-along manner. She felt the quiet silence and put her bag in her room. Then she started dinner. Michael would be home from school in a little while, to join them on his Christmas break. She cleaned the chicken breasts and poured cream of mushroom soup over them. After popping the pan in the oven, she went to the Christmas tree and sat down, gazing at it.

"I'm so happy we have a tree; I did it all myself, except dad putting it in the tree holder. I really am running our home; the folks pitch in helping with a couple of meals a week. Remember Mandy, doofus brain, mom and dad're still super creeped out about what I do," she spoke out. "But I'm getting a handle on all this; Owen listens super close to me, and what he says is pretty important. How'd he get so smart, for a kid?"

She hummed a Christmas carol, then sang out "O Christmas Tree," swaying back and forth. She hopped up and headed for the kitchen.

"Gotta get going, table to set, with our Christmas stuff. I'm so happy to see Michael soon. Love, Mandy, love them all, my family, the more I love, the more I want to love. I really care about Owen. He's so grown up. The couple other guys I've had dates with, seniors, but ick, so immature, just interested in grab ass."

She shook her head as she finished setting the table.

"Home, I'm home," she heard from the front door.

She walked through the great room, looking to her big brother. They hugged.

Michael stepped away from her, "When'd you get so beautiful, Sis?"

"Dunno, you told me that two years ago, after gran's reception, thanks for the compliment."

He whispered, "I know you don't get that from mom and dad."

"Yeah," she smiled up to him. "Hey, I brewed coffee, want some?"

"Uh huh, I'll take my gear to my room. What time's dinner."

"6, as always."

"I need to talk to you, guy/girl stuff."

"You're askin' advice from me, your little sis?"

"You're quite wise, I know."

∽

Mandy asked Owen to join her family Christmas afternoon. She wanted her folks to get to know this boy she liked. Before he arrived Michael asked to talk with Mandy.

"Sis, I'm kinda like you right now, met a cadet, we're both juniors. I need to know what I should do, from your viewpoint."

He sat at Mandy's desk chair in her room, and she sat on the floor, leaning against her bed. She looked up at him as he explained his situation.

"Not a lot of experience, but Michael, can tell you from what I've been through, each day's precious, if you love her, just love her. Let her know how you feel. We just've never gotten that from mom and dad, the touchy-feely kinda stuff. Matter of fact, you are the person in this family who's shown how you care; you've done that since you went away to school."

"It's 'cause I appreciate you, and the folks so much. And next year is it; I'll commission, then I'm pretty sure, 'cause I'll be in R&D, that I'll at least start at Wright Pat, and go from there."

"Uh, R&D?"

He nodded to her, "Research and Development."

"That's what I thought, and your friend, you said she thinks she's headed for pilot training?"

"Yup."

"Where'll that be?"

"Maxwell, for starters."

Mandy raised her knees and put her elbows on them, holding her head in her hands. She shook her head up to him.

"Yeah, I know what you're gonna say."

"Michael, you're in two very different occupations; you'll never match up, never get a chance to be together very much. You know you'll pretty much stay in your R&D placement, a lot of time in one location."

"Uh huh, and, if she makes it through pilot training," he paused, and let out a big sigh, "and she will, she'll be shipped all over the world. We're still in a Middle East conflict."

"My honest assessment, big brother, be her friend, love and care for her, but you gotta let her go. You might want to ease away soon. You got two semesters, then next spring, your assignments, graduation and you'll belong to the Air Force. Time'll go quick."

Mandy saw the tears in his eyes. She got up and came to him as she watched him drop his head. She put her arm around his shoulder and her other hand touching his cheek.

"I'm so sorry."

"So am I, thanks Mandy, I really appreciate what you just said."

She heard the doorbell, ran down the steps and let Owen in. She felt his warm strong hug.

"Oh, Merry Christmas, Owen," she smiled up to him.

"Merry Christmas, Mandy."

"I was glad to see you at the midnight service, with your family, just like two Christmas Eve's ago, uh and last Christmas Eve."

"Yeah, it's a tradition of ours. And your home," he paused and looked around the great room, "so decked out, in the holiday spirit, nice. Did you do all this, Mandy?"

"I did, including the tree."

She held his hand as they walked through the great room to the open kitchen, where her parents sat at the kitchen island. They stood and shook hands with Owen, their first formal introduction to him.

"Your folks, please wish them Happy Holidays from our family," Jim smiled to Owen.

"Will do," he nodded to Cindy and Jim.

"We saved dessert for your coming," Mandy spoke up, "and we'll each fix our own."

Michael joined them and shook hands with Owen.

"Wow, you just grow taller and taller."

"Yeah, my mom says it's my final growth spurt, trouble keeping me in long enough pants."

The parents laughed, "Oh, we remember that well, with Michael."

Everyone helped themselves to pumpkin pie and whipped cream. Then they gathered around the cozy fire. Mandy and Owen sat in chairs next to each other.

Michael got coffee for everyone and then sat opposite them. The parents settled on the couch. It was quiet for a little while, as they enjoyed the pie.

"Hey, you could hardly see that piece of pie for all the whipped cream."

Owen responded, "Uh huh, Mandy, the whipped cream is the most awesome part."

The family agreed, especially Michael.

"Owen," Cindy asked, "share about yourself."

He gazed around at this family, with his final gaze directed toward Mandy, sitting next to him. Owen gave them his background, shared that his third grade teacher was Mary Beth Overton, and his thoughts for the rest of high school.

"And after that?" Michael asked.

"Iowa Air Force National Guard," he nodded to Michael. "Mandy tells me about your upcoming officership, please, tell me about that."

"You first," Michael nodded.

"I want to serve my country. I'll go Air Guard as soon as I graduate, basic at Lackland, eight + weeks."

Jim asked, "How's your dad gonna cope with the corn harvest, without your help; I know lots of farmers work together at that time?"

"You're right, Jim, dad says he'll work it out, 'cause I'll be in a training school for weeks or months after basic."

"What's your specialty gonna be?"

"Don't know what they'll do with me; I know I want to be with the 185th Air Refueling Wing, at Sioux City Air National Guard Base." He nodded as he went on, "that's the KC-135R Stratotanker, where it's based."

"So you'll help with mid-air refueling and mobility sustainment to directly support the global mission of the Air Force."

"Exactly, Michael, we'll go wherever we're needed, you know, this war," Owen nodded.

"Oh my goodness," Cindy spoke out as she stood and helped take away plates. Mandy helped refresh coffee.

"Michael, you're a junior in the Air Force ROTC program at Iowa State, right?"

"Chemistry major, know I'll go R&D right away, what I'd like to end up doing is working on fuels projects."

"Uh huh, can't gas up another plane from the KC if we don't have the proper gas. One thing for sure, Michael, lots of work to be done on getting the cost of fuel down. Air Force can't survive without its fuel."

"You got it, Owen."

"Mandy, we'll give you some time with Owen."

Her parents and Michael left the great room for their bedrooms. They asked Owen to stay for cards, but he needed to get home, extra company this year, a girl coming home with Matt, his brother.

Owen took Mandy's hand and they moved to the couch, still warm from her parents' sitting there.

"Air Force for both of us, your brother and me. I guess it didn't sink in when you told me about Michael."

"I watched mom and dad as you two talked to each other. I know they're pleased; you both have great plans for your futures."

"They approve."

Mandy turned and looked into his eyes, "Yes, they do, for both of you. And I'm," she paused, "the outlier, the different one."

"I admire what you plan to do, Mandy."

"And do you approve?"

"I do; it'll be an awesome learning experience for us, as we both proceed on."

"Owen, you're important to me, and I really really like you. I want to get to know you better."

He put his arm around Mandy's shoulder, "And I want to get to know the inner Mandy, the girl who loves and loves, herself, God, her family, and loves the work she's doing, and wants to do."

"You don't talk about the corn, Owen, just the immediate Guard stuff. You've really thought it through, the farm, taking it over, your dad stepping away?"

"That's the AA in Ag Business, as quick as I can learn all of that. Dad's got me training on the books, the agriculture past, and some of the financing. It's a really big business, guess I didn't have any idea. In the 1990's dad got hold of a chunk of land, good time to do that, government helped some."

"So you have a lot of land, a lot of corn to plant and harvest?" she turned to him with her questioning eyes.

"Fer sure, gosh, it's a crazy time, harvest."

"So time wise, I'm thinkin' I'll probably be in my Mortuary Science internship about the time you finish your AA."

"You're right, but the Guard, do you know what that means after I get the basics out of the way?"

"No I don't.," she shook her head to him.

"Six years, one weekend a month, and two weeks a year of serving, out doing whatever Iowa needs us to do."

"Right, you guys, you're not regular Air Force, like Michael will be."

"That's right."

"But you could still get called up, to support the Air Force mission."

"It's a serious commitment, Mandy."

"And you and your mom and dad, have talked about all this?"

"Yeah, in great detail, they are proud of me, wanting to serve my country. It's somethin' I gotta do."

"Wow, you're committed. Thanks for sharing with me, Owen, my gosh the next five or so years of our lives are pretty much decided."

"It's quite a journey we'll take."

"I want to spend time with you, on that journey," she touched his upper arm.

They turned to each other. Mandy raised her lips up to him and he gave her a soft, caressing kiss. They moved their heads away from each other.

She smiled to him, "My best Christmas present."

He nodded, "And my best Christmas present."

3

2009 Christmas – Senior Year

"Do you remember my best Christmas present, last year on Christmas afternoon?"

"I do, a kiss we shared, our first kiss, what, oh gosh, a wonderful present we gave each other," Mandy smiled to Owen as she ran next to him at the high school track.

"You're runnin' great."

"Yeah, my every Sunday afternoon, when I can, runs kept me in shape, making my running time good. Besides, it's my natural high, like my feet aren't even touching the ground."

They ended their run, bending over to catch their breaths.

"I wish that's the way it is with me, Mandy, but for me runnin's always been hard work, no high at all."

"Maybe it's your much bigger body, more exertion needed to move your mass along."

"Could be," he stood up tall as Mandy did.

They hugged, side to side, their shirts matted down from their sweat.

"We're so lucky, the track, clear of snow, so we can run hard."

Mandy took his hand in her own as they walked along together.

"Tomorrow's Christmas Eve, on a Thursday, kinda an amazing three day weekend coming up."

"Yeah, I only had to go in for three hours this morning. But we got a funeral and reception on Monday, at the mortuary."

"Hey, that's a terrible time for the family of the person who's died."

"Owen, there's no good time, but the holidays are the worst, kinda explodes the emotions of the survivors."

He stood with her next to her car.

"And you'd know that better'n anyone; three years now?"

"That's right, in one sense, like yesterday, in another, a billion years ago."

"But what happened then, to your gran," he started to say.

She interjected, "Led me to today, and my future."

They hugged again, "You a part of the chorus that'll sing at the senior nursing facility tomorrow?"

"I am, for sure. I love doing that, last year and this year. The senior citizens, they really like us, and we sing Christmas stuff they all know. They join in. And do you know the best part?"

"Nah, what's that?"

"Some folks who never talk, who never seem to be aware, it's like when we're singing, they actually sing, takes them back, maybe to their early days. It's an amazing thing to watch. The nursing home staff, they just smile and nod their approval at what happens with their older singers."

"I'm so glad the chorus visits, sings, gives back, that way."

"Are you going to join me at the elementary school, to see how gran's tree is doing?"

"I am; I'll meet you there. I'd forgotten about what you mentioned a while back, what your gran's class wanted to do in memory of her."

"Well, this will be my first time checking the tree out. There's no snow on the ground right now, so I'll hopefully find the marker to identify the tree."

They walked along the sidewalk in front of the elementary school, the school they attended.

"Seriously, the school looks way different; a renovation, it looks like."

"Yeah, Mandy, I heard about that, kinda over two summers ago. Hey,

I bet this's it."

Mandy knelt down in front of a sturdy little oak tree. She brushed her hand over the bronze plaque, removing small leaves and twigs. Owen joined her, touching her upper arm and saying "Mrs. Mary Beth Overton, our teacher."

On the next line he read, "Her third grade class, 2006."

Mandy jumped up and away from the tree and plaque. Tears dribbled down her face as she had trouble breathing from all the liquid in her throat.

She gasped, "Oh gran, oh gran, I miss you so much."

She put her hands over her face and walked further back. Owen attempted to move close to her, to comfort her. She shook her head to him,

"I need a minute," she blurted out.

She took deep breaths, and it did help her calm down. After a little while Mandy walked back to the tree.

"What a beautiful little oak you are, you'll grow slow, but you'll grow strong."

Owen gave her a side-to-side hug, "Strong."

"Her grief is deep, so deep it only comes once in a while, now that some time's passed," Owen thought as he continued to hug her.

"Can't believe how hard that hit me, a living tribute to gran," she looked up into Owen's dark eyes.

"Would you like to come back?"

"Yeah, every year, at Christmas, every year I can come home. Gotta head out; Michael's with us, probably his last Christmas with the family."

"Yeah, same for me, with Matt coming home. Both our brothers've got just one semester left of school."

"Michael's so excited, hoping to work in research."

"Well, Matt doesn't have a job yet; he's been interviewing."

"See ya, Owen, I love you."

"And I love you."

They kissed and held on.

When they let go, Mandy mentioned, "once I get that funeral over, I'll really want to see you."

"Right, and I want to be with you. But this Christmas is for our big brothers."

℘

"I want to ride along with you, Sis. It'll be the last time I'll get to do this."

"Yeah, our lives move on. I won't be so far away, so I'll continue to do this."

Two days earlier Mandy created Christmas greenery for gran. She learned how to make the greenery from a video.

Mandy and Michael left their parents at home after the Christmas meal early in the afternoon of Christmas Day.

"We had a bit of snow. The greenery will look great against gran's grave."

"I like the way you did it, narrow and long, almost like a centerpiece, entwined with pine cones and fake red berries."

"Yeah, it is a centerpiece, to honor gran."

He carried the greenery, following Mandy as she found the Overton plot in the graveyard. He started to hand the greenery to her. She shook her head.

"I want you to do it, Michael, put it, like next to her gravestone. It'll be, possibly, the last time you'll do this with me."

Michael brushed the snow away from the bottom of the gravestone and placed the greenery there. He stood. Mandy held his hand, and they stepped back from the grave.

"It's beautiful, against the white snow and the gray stone. Gran, we love you."

Michael repeated, "We love you."

Mandy burst into tears. Michael hugged her as he started to cry. They stood together for several minutes.

"Oh gran, so many memories," Mandy's head swirled as her mind traveled through the years of memories with her gran.

Mandy wiped her eyes and nose with a tissue.

"You're with me always," Mandy whispered as she turned back one last time to view gran's gravestone.

℘

"Mandy, we saw you at midnight mass."

"Yeah, it was just Michael and me. My folks, they," she paused.

"It's OK, you don't have to explain. And Merry Christmas, this's my Christmas call. You and Michael were gone earlier in the afternoon."

"Uh huh, did my folks tell you we were at gran's grave?"

"They did."

"Michael wanted, maybe last time, to visit gran there. It was pretty emotional for both of us, been several years, can't believe it."

Owen and Mandy made plans to meet at his farm on the afternoon before New Year's Eve. Neither of them had any interest in the various football games showing on the networks.

℘

Owen ushered her in to the Northwood living room. She slipped off her boots and coat. They sat, having coffee and oatmeal raisin cookies at the kitchen table. His parents came by, from outside, to say hello to her and wish her a Happy New Year.

He looked down at her stocking feet, "Yeah, glad you brought your heavy boots, like I suggested. I want to take you for a walk around the home and surrounding area, somethin' I want to show you."

She felt an easy wind whisper across her face as she held hands with Owen. He gave her a tour of the Northwood property, around the home, to the back of the property, where the barn sat well away from the home.

"This looks like old barn wood," Mandy touched the weathered wood along the front entrance to the barn.

Owen touched her shoulder and nodded, "Good call, that's 'zactly what it is. Mom knew we had to take the aged barn down. So with helpers the barn got deconstructed, uh, fancy term for taking it down and using parts of the barn again, which we have."

"That's so great, saving the wood, from the olden days."

He opened a separate front door to the barn and walked with her into the middle area. She saw farm equipment parked on one side, and animals in stalls on the other side.

"Here's an office, and even a bathroom, for our help, especially at harvest."

"Nice, when did this happen?"

"Papow, my granddad, suggested it a couple of years before he died. He kinda supervised all the work; I was old enough to help out, kinda a helper on the project."

"How great, for you to know him, sort a like me knowing my gran."

"Uh huh, and after he died memaw lived with us for a short time, until she moved to town, to a nice apartment."

"She had enough of the farm life?"

"Uh huh, she's a social butterfly, so spends time with her friends. She comes out for some holidays, but just for a few hours. We're happy she has her own life."

Owen held her hand after they climbed over the rail fence that bordered both sides of the drive into the Northwood home. They walked through a small field. To the left of the field he led her into a grove of many trees, some oak and maple, and scattered evergreen trees.

In the middle of the tree area Mandy stopped and looked around and around.

"This area, it's so beautiful, even with no leaves on the trees. Were all these trees here from the old days?"

"Nah, my great granddad, he planted a lot of these. He wanted a feed crop, but he also wanted a small forest."

"Gosh, if he could see this, he'd be so pleased."

"I know he is," Owen stopped and looked up to the sky. Mandy watched him smile.

"Uh, let's keep going, Mandy."

He held her hand as they walked to a clearing.

"See the back area, it's one of our fields, and to the left, a few trees, and to the right, many trees."

She turned around, "Oh, there's kinda a trail coming into this area. And I can see the road, back in the distance."

"This is my 'come to' place, to think, to read, to plan. I didn't have much space for myself, part of my youth, had to share a room with Matt, until we built on to the house. What'cha think?"

"Awesome, a beautiful area, quiet, I even hear, is it a crow?"

"Yip, once in a while a crow flies through in the winter, mostly it's quiet, deer, see them on occasion."

Owen turned Mandy to him and put his hand under her chin, lifted it and gave her a soft feathery kiss. She kissed him back and stepped away from him for a moment.

"What does this all mean, Owen?"

"This 'come to' place, one day I want to build a home, right here. I love you, Mandy, and I want you to live here with me, you as my wife, and one day, our children."

"Oh Owen, for our someday," she nodded her head as tears blazed her eyes. She stepped back to him and put her arms up and around his shoulders. They kissed, again and again. His tears started and they had to let go of each other to clear their eyes and noses.

For several minutes they simply stood and smiled to each other.

"We're really young."

"Right, we are now, but Mandy, it's never been clearer to me that one day you will be the person I'll wake with every morning, for the rest of our lives. Your smile, my light, to guide me."

"If it's God's plan for us, Owen."

He nodded to her as he took her hand, "God's plan."

They hugged. Mandy looked about her at the trees, the openings clear of trees in front of her and in back.

"This's a wonderful area," she nodded and smiled up to Owen, "what a place you chosen!"

They held hands as they returned through the small forest to the Northwood land and home.

&

"Your poinsettia, such an awesome red. What made you decide you wanted that as your present this Christmas time?"

They sat next to each other at a table. It was a quiet place in the back of the Porttown library. Mandy came earlier on this New Year's Eve to work on a paper for her AP History class. It wasn't due for several weeks, but she wanted it completed, with studying and work coming.

"Do you know the poinsettia story, Owen?"

"Nah, so share."

"A young and poor little girl, living in Mexico, she wanted to give the Christ Child a gift. So her cousin came to her, about the dilemma she had and he told her that a gift, no matter how humble, if it was given in love, well, that would be a welcomed present for the Child. She found green weeds and took the bouquet to the foot of the creche where the tiny figure of the Christ Child lay, his parents gazing down at him. The girl watched the weeds burst into blooms of red. From that day on, the poinsettia has also been known as the Flower of the Holy Night, that's Christmas Eve for us."

"Wow, Mandy, a gift given with love."

"Now you know, given in love."

She leaned to the side and kissed his cheek.

"That cousin, he was a wise young man."

Mandy nodded to him.

"So why am I here, Mandy?"

"I need your advice."

"Well, you've called me wise before, not sure that's accurate, but what's this?"

She placed a packet of blue envelopes, tied with a red ribbon, in front of him.

"Please read these; to my knowledge, no one else's ever looked at them 'cept me and gran."

"OK, but the background?"

He looked at her, frown lines on her forehead, and brown eyes turning darker.

"From my Granddad Overton to my gran. Yip, I'll work on the paper, and let you read."

Twenty minutes later Owen laid his hand flat over the open pages, the envelopes set to one side. He put his other hand to the side of his head and rubbed his head.

"Man, my brain's spinnin', your grandparents," he looked into Mandy's eyes and shook his head.

"Yeah, gran came to me a couple nights back, and whispered to read the letters, that's all she said."

"Gran, she still visits you?"

"Now, just a voice, but it's her voice."

"How the heck did you get these?"

"Cleanin' out a drawer in gran's room, at the bottom of the drawer with all her pretty underthings, you know, right after she died and we had to put her home up for sale."

"Does anyone else know about these letters or this situation?"

Mandy shook her head to him, a teary look in her eyes.

"Whispers, soft talk now, OK?" she asked him.

He nodded to her and put his finger on his lips.

"I don't know, Owen, it's pretty, nope, I can't judge."

"That's right, Mandy, neither can I judge. But it's kinda unbelievable, your granddad, still married to gran, and your uncle, both in sexual relationships with this woman, at the same time. She was?"

"A music teacher, private lessons, piano, voice; she was beautiful, sang and acted in community theater in Porttown. She left town."

"And a baby, oh Mandy, I bet nobody's told your mom and dad."

"I hope not; it'll kill my dad."

"I hate to say anything, but God must'a been in this plan. He took the baby to heaven, to maybe spare total heartache. I just can't imagine, a woman doing something like this, like who's the father? Your granddad and uncle, I can't even wrap my head around this. I gotta let go of this information."

"Owen, I really think gran just took this to her grave, never explaining the split with granddad, the split with her other son."

"Yeah, it's like, three people've died, gran, your granddad, and your uncle."

"Right, no communication, a lot of years now, but I did call granddad when gran died. He thanked me and said he'd get a message to my uncle. But, well I understand, neither of them showed up for her celebration."

"So, Mandy, you got a plan for your life, what do you want to do about this?"

"Keep it to myself, only you know, and 'course, granddad and uncle. And I'll never say anything to my folks. But, since the sadness may be fading from all this, I'm gonna send granddad my graduation announcement, and invite him to come. Michael did not send him an invitation, but that was a while ago, and the wounds were raw from my grandparents splitting up."

Mandy helped him fold the letters and put them back in the proper dated envelopes. He reached his arm across the back of her chair and hugged her.

"You've known about this for a little bit; I hope you didn't dwell on this, Mandy."

"It bothered the heck out of me for a few months after gran died, wondering and wondering, but I did let it go, until gran asked me to read the letters. Can tell you from what little I've learned at the mortuary that many kinds of unbelievable craziness happen to families. And stuff comes out at the death of a loved one. I just feel bad, for what happened to my grandparents, and uncle. Owen, is sexual attraction, is it just that powerful?"

Mandy watched him nod his head, "I really think it is, but it's sexual attraction, and I don't think love."

"The way I feel about you, Owen, I love you, and one day I want to have sex with you, but, we've got respect, and we've got caring, and that goes a long ways."

"Same for me, Mandy, tougher for guys, sexual want, sometimes so strong. Confess, I'm not a virgin, exciting, but just an act, feeling like I'd been used."

"Wow, Owen, oh gosh."

They held hands for a little while before they needed to leave the library.

"What you gonna do with the letters?"

"Get them back to granddad, right away by mail. I don't want my folks ever seeing them. If he actually comes to graduation, I hope to be able to spend a little time with him. Shame is also a powerful force, and I suspect granddad feels a lot of that, especially since gran's gone. And Owen, thank you for listening to me and reading through the information. It was some pretty tough stuff."

"Really was, this stays with me, just you and me know. It's gotta stay that way, right?"

He watched her nod to him, her eyes bright and shining into his, "That's right."

℃

"I can't believe I'm waltzing with you," Mandy smiled up to Owen as they moved around the dance floor of the hotel ballroom.

"You are, and I'm so happy being with you, holding you close for the slow dances."

"This is my first and only prom. In my wildest dreams, I never thought I'd come, or be able to be with a guy I cared for."

"From the girl talk I hear, it is the highlight of many a young lady's high school experience, just sayin' from cross country and conversations I run into."

He held her close in the next to last dance of the evening.

"Mandy, you light me up, give me hope and confidence in my future."

She whispered up to him, "I love you; you give me courage, and joy."

"We'll only get to have special times together, for the next few years, but my love for you's not gonna change, Mandy. It's steadfast. I want you to see other guys, as you've asked me to see other women."

"That's right, in a couple of years, after we've been out of our sheltered teen world and into the military and academic worlds, that's when we'll know, us coming together, a more mature love."

$\wp$

Mandy liked Michael's commissioning ceremony much more than his graduation ceremony from Iowa State. She felt a bit in awe of all the uniformed students, officers, and military personnel at the commissioning. Michael never spoke much about the military aspect of his college work. After the official commissioning ceremony a cake and punch reception took place in the back part of the ballroom where the cadets commissioned. Michael introduced his mom, dad, and Mandy to various officers and the new 2nd lieutenants, his friends, men and women who went through the Air Force ROTC program together.

Mandy stepped back away from the group. She watched the new officers' smiles and genuine sounds of happiness to be moving on with their lives and beginning their military careers.

"I've just seen too much, already," she thought to herself, as she remembered, "Yeah, I've helped with the funerals, back in Porttown, of two different young men, military officers, who did not survive the conflict we're in right now. Their funeral ceremonies, so filled with military tradition, the draped casket, in one case, a 21-gun salute, oh goodness, Mandy."

She exhaled a large breath and began to move toward her family, seated at a table.

"Go get cake, Sis; coffee's good."

Mandy got in line to get punch, cake, and mixed nuts. She balanced coffee in one hand and cake in the other as she returned to the table.

"You know I won't be able to see you graduate."

"I understand, Michael, pretty sure that would happen. But I wanted to be here for all this. Maybe one day I can visit and see my lab rat brother working on some exotic project."

Michael patted her shoulder, "That would be my hope, Sis."

∽

"We'll do the same special after-graduation for Owen as we did for Matt."

"That's right, Brad, it's important; they're different boys, but I want that to be something equal for both of them," Sara nodded to her husband as they stood together, preparing dinner.

"And somethin' else, Mandy's folks don't plan to have anything special for Mandy, that's what Owen told me. The one set of grandparents cannot attend. But, her Granddad Overton is coming to her graduation, the first time he's visited since his split with Mandy's grandmother. I think that's been a few years ago."

"Mandy's really wonderful, and Owen's over the moon for her. I'm going to check in with Cindy Overton, and tell her we'd like to honor Mandy as well as Owen, in our celebration."

"Do it, Sara, all Owen's said is that Mandy's relationship with her folks's been strained for years, Mandy wanting to do a different path with her life, the mortuary science after her AA."

∽

"Graduation, are you gettin' ready?" Sally Ann asked her friend as they left school that late May afternoon.

Mandy headed for her car and her afternoon at the mortuary.

"Yeah, I'm pretty sure I got everything under control, start Monday after we graduate, at the Ankmer community college campus.   And I'm helping Sara Northwood with the graduation party for Owen and me. You got your invitation, right?"

"Uh huh, did, and I'm coming, so this is my RSVP. It's so nice they're including you; they're super special folks, and I know they really care about you, Mandy."

Mandy nodded her head, "For sure, blessed am I."

They stood by Mandy's car.

"A place to live at school?"

"Yeah, girl, nice, complex with units of three bedrooms with private bathrooms for each, common kitchen, dishwasher, dining area with a small living room, washer and dryer. So I'll have a couple of roommates."

"Far from campus?"

"Nope, right next door, I'll hardly use my car much."

"See you, Mandy, hey, why the Ankmer campus?"

"A big campus, that's where I'll get my AA, and that's where the Mortuary Science program's offered."

"Good for you."

"And you?"

"Gonna work this summer; try to get my head around what I might want to do, still feel aimless. Wish I had your vision; you got everything planned out."

They hugged before they left the school parking lot.

As Mandy drove away she spoke out, "Gran, you've helped me so much; my guide, making me decide to study hard, make good grades, which I'll have to continue.   And because of what I do, helping at the mortuary, I've learned time management skills, getting my studying done, run a home, work.   Swear I'll have time on my hands when I get to community college (cc), after everything I've done."

She broke into a Christmas song, "Mary's Boy Child," a song her choir sang at the school holiday concert at Christmas, and at the senior home.

ဆာ

"Thank you for coming, Granddad."

"I appreciated the invitation. And being able to stay with you and your folks, in Michael's old room, well, it's nice."

They met up with Mandy's folks after the ceremony.

"It was a special ceremony, Mandy; your choir's rendition of "We've Only Just Begun," it was heartfelt," Cindy hugged her daughter. Her dad patted Mandy's shoulder after Mandy stepped away from her mom.

"I agree," her dad spoke up, "and ranking third in your class, well, we didn't know, a surprise, and we're real proud of you."

Mandy's mind swirled as she thought back, "I haven't heard the word proud from you, since gran's death."

"Thanks, Dad."

"Shall we take two cars to the Northwood party?"

"Good idea, Granddad, ride with me?"

"Great."

The parents agreed to meet Mandy and her granddad at the Northwood reception. They first needed to take care of a matter needing attention at home.

Mandy began as soon as they drove away from the school parking lot.

"You got the letters?"

"I did, no idea that Mary Beth would hang on to them. I read through all the letters. For the rest of my days, my anger, guilt, shame, discouragement will swirl around me. I made a mistake that cost me my family, home and community. I have a sadness, a mental depression about what I did, with that woman, to your grandmother, my son, to a baby I guess I'll only meet one day, in heaven, if God decides."

"Granddad, only gran, you, Uncle Justin, as far as I know, have knowledge of this. I did share with Owen, because I didn't know what to do about this information. Gran appeared to me once, before her funeral celebration, and she's spoken to me twice, since I found the letters as Michael and I got her place ready to sell. So what's happened, it goes with me, and Owen, I'm sure, to our graves."

"Mandy, I think it's something that ate on your grandmother, for years, helped cause her stress, that could have contributed to the horrible heart attack that took her."

"Right, and mom and dad, not ever necessary to."

Her granddad cut in, "Say anything to them. Justin'll stay quiet. They got so much stress on them, part of the year, assessor's office, and county clerk's, those are tough jobs."

Mandy parked along the road, seeing that the lane into the Northwood home filled with cars parked along either side of the road. They stood looking at each other before they walked up the road.

"I'm very proud of you, Mandy, for all you've accomplished, asking me to come. Jim is being very pleasant with me. And to tell you," he took her hand and held it to his cheek, "you are beautiful, so different looking from your parents, truly just you."

They held hands as they walked along. Mandy turned to him.

"And Granddad, you are still unbelievably handsome, gran, so lovely, I'm sure you two turned a few heads when you were together."

"Yeah, our friends called us a perfect match."

"Are you ready?"

"Let's go in and celebrate you and Owen."

Mandy gazed around at the decorations she and Sara put up the afternoon before. Banners and stars were kept from Matt's celebration at his graduation years before. The Overton family paid for and had a special cake delivered later that same afternoon. That and the cans of pop and ice tea completed their help with the food for the celebration. Sara and Brad contributed finger food and the plates, plastic ware, and napkins. Tablecloths and napkins blended into the school colors, vibrant purple and gold.

Mandy stood by herself for a little while, tears in her eyes.

"This turned out so special; oh, many people care, to be here with us."

Owen found her, and they hugged.

"Mandy, awesome, most of the cross country team, and your choir are here. Do ya think, maybe your group could sing a song or two?"

"Hey, we definitely can do that."

And they did. A few minutes later the choir sang "We've Only Just Begun" and "Climb Every Mountain." They held hands and swayed from left to right as they sang. Mandy looked up after she sang, "For you gran, we really are special, don't you think?"

She did not get a reply, but for the rest of that celebration Mandy felt filled up with the warmth of joy and a sense of accomplishment.

4

Summer 2010

"I'm glad I drove my car to help you out, Mandy."

"You can get back as soon as I get my stuff hauled to my place."

Cindy helped Mandy with three loads from each car. That took care of everything Mandy wanted to bring.

"Nice," Cindy looked around at the apartment. "You'll eventually have two roommates, is that right away?"

"Not sure, Mom, I'd a thought one roommate might be here, with classes starting tomorrow. But summer school is real different, with classes for various periods of time, and also times of the day and evening."

"Your books?"

"Tomorrow, in between classes, I'll pick them up at the campus bookstore."

"You told me, you've tested out of history and math?"

"That's right, my AP classes at Porttown High, this cc, they're giving me credit, 'cause I passed the AP classes and final AP exams with flying colors."

"What's it mean, later on?"

"If I work real hard, Mom, I'll graduate at the end of next summer with my AA. It'll be great, because tuition here is less expensive than at the four year schools. Then I hope I'll be admitted and start on my Mortuary Science program in the fall. But that'll be three very tough semesters, with an internship of over a month or so, during my final term."

"Well, I agree about the less expense; I hadn't thought about that with you. But I know how much we had to pay for Michael at Iowa State. Gran's money went fast for him. But for you, between what we've saved and gran's contribution, you should have no college loans to pay back when you're finished."

"That's correct, I did the calculations a while ago."

"Walk me out, Mandy, you really know what you want. You've kept your dream alive, all this time."

"I'll continue to keep heading to my goal."

They hugged at Cindy's car.

Mandy stepped back from her mom, "I love you, Mom, tell Dad I love him."

Cindy took Mandy's hand, "We love you, Mandy."

Mandy watched her mom get in her car, wave to her and drive away.

Tears came to Mandy's eyes, "Wow, can't even remember the last time my mom said that she loved me, her and dad."

She turned and hurried into her apartment, to get ready for school starting the next morning.

ઠာ

"Thank you for coming back. Have you been home?"

Mandy nodded to Sara, "Just before I came to your farm; my first time coming back to Porttown. I started at cc the week after graduation last May. I'm here to help out for the weekend. I gotta drive back tomorrow evening."

"Good, we need you. Without Owen's help, sheez, we never realized how much he did to help out, even when he was in school."

"I think, uh huh, he took several days off from high school to help out."

"He may have; the years just blur by me."

Mandy helped Sara with the preparation and serving of lunch and dinner on Saturday and would help Sunday with meals and several vehicle exchanges, to provide enough drivers to get the corn to the proper destination. Late Saturday evening she finally got away from the Northwood farm to head home for a shower and to go to bed. Her parents sat in the kitchen with her for a few minutes, before they retired.

"How's harvest going?"

"Oh, Mom and Dad, they have it down, a real science now, and they're helping out another family with their harvest. They say it's gonna be a good year."

She watched her dad nod to her, "If it's good for the corn farmer, then it will be good for our community, that's very nice news."

"Yeah, you heard it from a corn helper's mouth," she grinned to her folks.

Her parents laughed and caught her up in their sounds.

"And you, school still good?"

"Right, going great, almost half way done, I could almost do it in the spring semester, but my advisor says it's too big a load. And he wants me to have the great grades needed for the mortuary program. I will have a big challenge in the summer, taking my anatomy class, been advised to complete that before I start the mortuary program."

"Sounds like you had a good plan, to stay at the same school as you advance on."

"Uh huh, other cc campuses don't have the anatomy I need, gonna work out just great."

"Owen?"

"Still in training; he wants to work on the KC's at Sioux City, so he's getting quite a mechanic's background. He loves it, loves the Air Guard, much more satisfactory than he could've expected."

"Mandy, we're very glad to hear that. Michael also really likes what he's doing in research and his location, Wright Patterson Air Force Base."

Mandy nodded to her folks, "I c'n remember, that's really where he wanted to be stationed."

"To bed for us; to let you know, it sounds like Michael's going to deploy, for a time, location not determined, and we might not know," Jim nodded.

Mandy looked from parent to parent, "You knew that might happen, based on the kind of research Michael may be doing."

"Right, oh, use the washer and dryer."

"Thanks, I'll get started, I probably won't get back here, will drive to Ankmer from the Northwood's tomorrow."

"Thank you for helping them, Mandy, it's a gracious gesture, with Owen not available."

Mandy got up and hugged her parents, "I want to learn everything I can about corn harvesting."

They nodded to her and wished her goodnight.

While her clothes washed and dried Mandy showered and then sat with her textbooks on the floor of her room. The carpeted bedroom floor at school became her preferred place to study, except when she went to the cc library at night. There she sat in the quiet, in a cubbie, without distractions.

"Gotta keep running," she told herself as she drove back to school after helping out with harvest.

"I'm glad I could help out, with the crop. That won't happen after I get into the mortuary program. I'm so glad I went and talked with them. I like the program head. She's no nonsense, and she gave me important tips about getting in, and staying in the program. Some students, well, it's much different, than they expected, once they get in."

⁓

Mandy began volunteering at Ankmer Memorial Hospital the next week after corn harvest. She explained her future plans, what she'd done in high school for work. And when the volunteer coordinator asked her, she jumped at the chance to do the Saturday morning 8-10 shift nobody wanted. Mandy completed the TB tests she had to have, got the necessary flu shot, and finished the training program with the ER volunteer coordinator. She bought her volunteer shirt, a bright green, with Volunteer on one side of the collared polo shirt. And on the other side Ankmer Memorial Hospital was printed. Blue jeans were not allowed, so she wore white slacks and white tennis shoes with bright green shoestrings. Memorial did a background check on her, and she sent the two required letters of reference to the volunteer coordinator.

"What'cha think?" the ER charge nurse asked her as she finished up her first Saturday morning working by herself.

"Good," Mandy smiled and gave the nurse her bright smile.

"Wow, not what I expected to hear, usually the volunteer's ready to quit."

Mandy explained her background, the corpses she worked with, the families with blinding grief.

"So you're really aware of what we try to do, bring folks back to health."

"Right, and I'm sure lots of folks walk out of here, doing super better than when they walked in."

She watched Mona, the charge nurse, nod in agreement, "That's what we're tryin' for; you get it, cleanin' and making up beds, keeping the warming machines filled with blankets, general gopher work. You may guide family members, like to the cafeteria, or the pharmacy, or maybe just sit quiet with them. Is it like what you did, with the deceased's family?"

"Uh huh, 'cept, with those folks, hope's gone, there's a finality. It's not like here, where lots of patients still have an opportunity to have some quality of life."

"You've seen lots of grieving."

"I'm plannin' on completing the Mortuary Science program here at the Ankmer cc."

"So you'll see lots more sadness," she paused and looked into Mandy's eyes, "thanks for being here, Mandy."

"You'll find me here every Saturday morning," she nodded to the nurse.

"We welcome you; it's a tough shift, with the still sobering-up drunks, and people shot, cut up, vomiting, coming off their drugs from their Friday night good times. Oh my goodness, Mandy, it's not always like that."

"Gotcha," Mandy smiled to her.

ℴ⃝

That Christmas Mandy's folks spent the holiday with Cindy's parents in Ohio. She stayed back in Porttown and helped out with a life celebration at the mortuary. Her parents put up a tree, but did no other holiday decorating. The Northwood's asked her to join them at midnight service and for Christmas dinner the next afternoon. Matthew and memaw would be coming.

Mandy asked, and Sara agreed, to bring a ham as part of her contributing to the meal. Owen and his group were on a deployment, helping out on a critical out-of-state construction project that needed to get finished, so much so that the Air Guard got called in to assist. Mandy and Owen only talked by cell phone since the May before, when they graduated.

Memaw checked in with Mandy, after the dinner. They stood, helping put a brownie on each plate, then a scoop of vanilla ice cream over the brownie.

"He loves you very much, Mandy."

Mandy turned to memaw, "Oh I know, and absence sure's makin' my heart grow fonder. I don't know for certain when I'll see him 'cause he's starting at the cc in Charter right after the new year."

"That's if they get the construction project finished, that the Guard's helping with."

"Uh huh, he's sure hoping he can start on time with school."

"Me too, ah, these desserts look awesome, Mandy, shall we let folks put on the whipping cream they may want on top of all this?"

"Let's."

Mandy and memaw carried the desserts to the table. She heard aaahhh's and yummy coming from the family. The discussion among them all was always corn, and getting set up for the next corn crop. They talked about prepping the ground that April, and planting always arrived as a surprise, never enough time to get ready for it. Moisture, and then warming up of the soil, that was ever present in the minds of all farmers.

"Sara, you haven't talked about the library," Mandy asked.

"I love working there, have the three and four-year-old story time on Tuesday mornings. It's an absolute blast to see the wonder of little children."

Matthew shared his plan to start the Peace Corps in several months.

"I've been super dissatisfied with the work I'm doing, thinkin' my major of political science isn't gonna pan out. I'm just super lucky to have kept up my Spanish, all through high school, and at the university. I'll need that skill as I work in the small towns, with their water needs."

"Where'll you be sent?"

"Unknown, as of right now, except it'll be a Spanish-speaking country, at least I'm hoping," he smiled to his family.

Mandy headed away from the farm early that evening, exhausted from the school term and helping with the meal. She and Owen talked, wishing each other Merry Christmas.

"Cheez, this is what it's like out in the real world. Mandy, like I planned I'm hoping I can start classes at the cc in Chartner on time. It'll be a real pleasure to just be able to go to class and study."

"Think you'll be OK down the road, the corn farmer, and still the Guard one weekend a month, and then the two weeks once a year?"

"That'd be nice; 'cept the deployments are always possible. Yeah, it's what I signed up for, and for you?"

"School's good; volunteering's good. Spring and summer're gonna be fast. I'm applying to Mortuary Science when I get back. I stopped by one day between classes. The program chair happened to be there and talked with me for a minute. Most important thing I'll do is take that anatomy class this summer. It's offered on the Ankmer campus. She says that's what throws off many applicants. Some don't pass anatomy wherever they take it."

"They can't get into the program."

"Right, Owen, I think then's when they realize what's really gonna happen, the human body, after all, is what this's all about."

"But you really understand."

"I do, so again, I'm so glad I worked at the mortuary in high school. Otherwise, a person has no idea how strong emotions are, in the loss of a loved one. Other thing the woman told me is the dropout rate after graduation. She was super blunt; one in two, after just a short time, leaves the field. It's just too much, for a person's emotions. And the work can be 24/7, and then gaps, until the next event. Plus, you gotta be strong. I'm lifting weights. Heaving around corpses is very heavy work."

"How was Christmas dinner with my family?"

"Wonderful, your memaw, a character, and your bro seems happy with his Peace Corps plans, and 'course, your mom and dad, honestly, the most solid and common sense people I've ever met. You got your training from good folks."

"Now, more than ever, I understand that. Some of the people in my group, shish, the stuff they share, well, about their folks. You know how lucky we are to have good parents?"

"I do, some of the stuff, maybe like my gran and granddad?"

"Yip, even more bizarre than their situation was."

"We'll keep in touch, Owen, through this coming spring semester. I'm glad you got a place in student housing next to campus. After your military experience, it'll be nice to be a college student for a time."

"I'm a little concerned; just having to go to class and study. I sure did a lot of night studying in my training. Now I'll learn the theory and practical parts of agribusiness."

"It'll apply to everything you do on the farm."

"I'm glad dad's been training me for the past few years. I'm hoping to learn tips to make it all better for us, as I take over the operation."

"I think it's so important. Yeah, and you need the college experience, Owen, to meet people your own age, to have fun when you can. You know I want you to date, to meet all kinds of girls."

"And the same for you, Mandy, are you seeing anyone?"

"There's a group of us, three girls and two guys, who kinda hang together. They're fun and not ready to date. Two of us plan on the mortuary science program. What about for you?"

"Kinda like you, only a couple of females in our group, we'll probably do stuff together once in a while. But we'll soon be scattering, a couple going on to school, like me.

"I'm glad that you are getting out a little bit."

"I love you, Mandy, everything's seems to be going good for you."

"And for you Owen, I hope they let you go. You'll start classes with the rest of your group. I love you, Owen."

"Happy New Year."

"Happy New Year, Owen."

2011

Spring and summer semesters blurred along at a furious pace for both Owen and Mandy. Summer term began the Monday after the spring final exams the Friday before. The cell phone became the lifeline between them.

"I'm on track to graduate, get the AA in August."

"What about anatomy?"

"It's hard, but I still gotta make time to study for my other classes. Oh, Owen, I made it in, to the Mortuary Science program, provided I pass anatomy. I got the physical they wanted completed, plus a couple of psych questions. And I showed them I could lift 50 pounds without a problem. I still have to have an interview, to make sure, you know, that I'm someone who can handle the emotional side of what I'll do."

"That's awesome, Mandy, 'course you'll pass anatomy, you are wicked smart."

"Thanks for that vote of confidence. Hey, do you have a break at all after summer classes before your fall term begins?"

"Three days, hey, our teachers, they don't mess around, all the students are under time pressure to finish up the agribusiness AA; they need to get on to farms, jobs, starting at universities for some of them."

"When're you due to finish?"

"I got summer, fall, spring 2012, graduate, AA done, then I'll concentrate on the farm."

"Maybe we can spend time together, during that three day break after summer; my mortuary course work starts at Ankmer at the same time as your fall class starts at the Chartner cc."

"Let's try, no promise, 'cause I haven't done my two weeks duty with Air Guard. I'm thinkin' it'll happen at Christmas time,' he sighed, "again."

℘

She set her bag down. They ran into each other's arms as she watched him come to her. They held on tight, standing in the sunlight of the Northwood front yard. Then they stood back from each other, holding onto each other's hands.

"The light in your eyes," he paused and let out a deep breath, "for me, Mandy," he nodded.

"Wow, Owen, time and the military've been good for you."

"I'm not that scrawny runner anymore," he smiled down to her.

"Me neither, runnin's been great for me, all this time, helped me with my weight training, if you can believe that."

"I can."

They came to each other again. He picked her up, swung her around and set her down. They gave each other gentle, caressing kisses, for all those months away from each other.

"Let's go say hi to your folks."

"They been expecting you. And they know you can't help with harvest this year, with your load at school."

"Yeah, I shared that with them after we had Christmas dinner together last year."

"I won't be able to help either, the middle of a practicum, for that fall class."

"Last year that your dad's gonna have to go it alone; next year, you'll be doin' it all."

"That's my hope."

He held her shoulder and carried the bag into the Northwood home.

She greeted Sara and Brad with hugs. She watched their eyes; she felt caring, lots of caring for her in their bright eyes and welcome response to seeing her.

"We're going to my place, Mom and Dad. I want to show Mandy what I've gotten done."

"Have fun; you'll be staying with your folks tonight, Mandy?"

"Uh huh, then back to Ankmer, to start my program. I'm very excited."

She saw Brad nod to her, "You're certainly in our thoughts and prayers, as you accomplish that goal of Mortuary Science. It's a special field, one meant for you."

"Thank you, that's what I'll need, especially your prayers."

"You two have fun on your picnic," Sara said.

Owen carried an old plaid blanket for sitting on, plus sparkling cider, cookies and chips. They held hands as they walked through the small field, the forest, and then the clearing.

He let go of her hand so she could walk ahead. He watched her set down the bag and walk, around and around, looking down at the concrete walls and flooring of a basement, along with the French drains dug down and outside the walls.

"Oh my gosh, Owen, you are, for reals, building yourself a home. I can see where you'll put in basement windows, to bring in light."

"What'cha think?"

"Unbelievable, how, how've you been able to do this?"

"Profits on my corn fields, after the corn's come in, sock it into stuff for the home."

"You gotta have a couple year plan."

"I do."

They sat on the blanket on the ground in the area that would be the backyard of the home. She looked ahead, then pointed with her arm, "Owen, what a beautiful view, out the front window?"

"That's right, but from every window it'll be a lovely sight outside."

"With the trees in the distance, and some we'll plant close."

"So I've kept myself busy, every second I can get here. My first commitment, like yours, is school, learn everything I can to better myself as a businessman farmer."

"Like I'm gonna do as a mortician funeral director."

He turned to her, "Never heard you say it like that."

"It's what I want to be. There's business and law involved, so many rules about mortician's work."

"Hungry?"

"Yeah, and thirsty, I'll dig out the chicken breasts and baked beans."

"And I'll pour out some cider in our cups, chips, and of course, cookies."

"Yip, for our sweet tooths."

They sat together, watching the sun submerge into the trees to the west.

"So good, what do you do with the chicken breasts?"

"Just some flour and my special rub on the breasts, pop them into the olive oil and fry them up, easy, peasy."

"Yeah, for you, I'd screw up every part of that."

He gave Mandy an ugly face, and they laughed together.

"I'm an excellent cook; I'll make sure your food always tastes yummy."

"Yeah, for sure, I know I'll love your cookin', and these baked beans, so sweet."

"A little brown sugar."

"Yyyuuummm."

They ate and drank and stuffed themselves.

"Two little piggies," Owen smiled to her as he rubbed his full tummy.

"Well, we about wiped out everything," Mandy giggled to him, "incredible."

They put away the little food that was left over and poured themselves more sparkling cider.

"Still trouble with alcohol?"

"Still, the smell, even of beer, or champagne, makes me want to barf."

"Down the road, will you be OK if I have a beer now and again?"

"Course, my problem is sure as heck not yours."

They sat looking up at the sky as it darkened. Mandy pointed out an outstanding bright star as it emerged from the cloud.

"Mandy," he paused and held her hand, "time-wise, our calendars, and this is sure not romantic. I want to marry you, at Christmas, before you start your funeral service practicum, last semester."

"I'd love that, Owen, I want to marry you. And I've been thinkin' about the same thing, a little afraid to say anything to you, until now. Your schoolwork, is it still going along good?"

She moved her face close to his. And as he nodded she turned and kissed his cheek. She watched him look straight ahead, studying the darkened scene.

"That'll mean a fall with you in your last full semester, me done, then spring, you at your mortuary internship, and me, here, getting the ground ready for planting, and preparing our home."

"Christmas, it'll be perfect. Knowing that I'll be finishing up; it'll be just a few months, and I'll be in state somewhere, then we'll be together, for always and forever, oh Owen."

They kissed and kissed, caressing each other for all those months they were apart. Mandy felt sharp throbbing pierce through her groin area. It intensified and began to move up and up, to her throat. They lay, side to side as they explored each other. He placed her hand on his engorged penis as they continued to kiss.

"I'm so moist, Owen," she whispered, "so ready to greet you."

He rolled on top of her, groaning, "And I'm so ready to greet you, but not now, not today. Don't have a condom, and I want us to think about birth control pills, in a few months. We haven't talked that through."

She held him tight against her, rubbing his back over his shirt.

"Wow, we really gotta deal with that. I don't want a surprise baby."

"And neither do I; you want to get your career off the ground."

"I do."

"I love you, Mandy. I want what's best for both of us."

"Thank you for that."

He raised himself up and lay down next her. They looked up at the stars.

"We're like a couple of 15 year olds, like what do we do next?" Mandy laughed and caught Owen up in the humor.

They sat up and gave each other a soft kiss.

"Time to head back?"

"Getting dark."

"Hey, I brought a trusty flashlight."

"You're so awesome, Owen, thinkin' of everything."

ℰℴ

Mandy drove home for the Thanksgiving break. Her mind whirled around the past two semesters in her Mortuary Science program. She shook her head as she remembered getting the Hepatitis B shots early in her first semester of her program. Several students neglected to get their shots. They got removed from the coursework, putting them behind in their program. They failed to realize that working with removing blood and body fluids and replacing them with embalming solution remained a health issue for an embalmer.

She spoke out as she drove along, "I gotta concentrate on my school work, plus helping Owen with the wedding plans. We'll keep it very simple, with the family-only church wedding ceremony, then the reception at our home."

"Dude, plus then heading for my funeral services practicum, yeah Mandy," she told herself, "so lucky to get placed at the fine funeral home the Hoskisson's recommended in Des Moines."

She remembered that five students from Mandy's class sought placement at this particular home. She started to bring in her bags.

"And I'm pretty sure I got placed there because I have high school experience plus've helped out at the mortuary when they got jammed up the last couple semesters. Hoskisson's wrote me a stellar recommendation letter."

Mandy remembered her interview several weeks earlier with the Danier mortuary folks.

"I's sure surprised," she noted to Owen in a call to him after her interview, "at the kinds of questions they asked about emotions, pain and sadness, in myself, and what I saw with grieving clients. If I hadn't had all those funeral experiences, being in the office, helping at receptions, prepping for funerals, I'd a never known how to answer their questions. Thank the Lord I worked in the business in high school. That's actually really saved me."

"Proud of you, my dear, you ignored your parents and went on about your business. You had to be so strong-willed."

"Yeah, Owen, thanks, stubborn, I think I know how to go about getting what I want."

He gave her a laugh, "That's for sure."

She came back to the present from remembering that conversation as she trudged with her bags to her bedroom.

"Last Thanksgiving in my parent's home; nice that we're inviting Owen, his parents, and his memaw," she spoke out as she returned to the kitchen.

℘

Owen stayed at the Overton home for a while longer after his folks departed that Thanksgiving afternoon. He stood in the kitchen, drying the last of the pans Mandy washed up. Owen pressed the start button on the dishwasher. Then he joined Mandy at the kitchen island. He drank the coffee she just poured for him. They heard cheers from the great room as Mandy's folks watched a favorite team in the football game.

She turned to him and touched his cheek.

"I love you so, not much waiting left," she smiled to him.

"Soon, I love you, Mandy," he paused, "how's the planning seem?"

"Well, you're in charge, since you live here, share."

"Reception invitations mailed out, caterer, minister, florist, all squared away. We have to sit down with our completed pre-nup homework and go over it together, and then meet reverend two days before we get married."

"Reception's mostly for our parents."

"Right, family, your grandparents, the Gregsons, memaw, and the rest, our folks' friends, just a few of our personal friends."

"Mostly your friends, Owen, 'cause I've been away, for almost four years now."

Owen scooted his stool closer to her.

He spoke in a soft voice, "Handling the birth control pills OK?"

She answered him in the same soft tone, "Yeah, just have to make sure I take the pill when I'm s'posed to, along with my daily vitamin and Vitamin C. "

"But feelin' OK, no reaction?"

"None that I can tell; I sure feel better," she whispered, "baby when we want to, after my career gets going."

"You got a room, for during the weeks when you're in Des Moines?"

"Yes, a bedroom and bathroom in rooming house, some interns who work for state legislators, they also live there. I'll get in on some interesting conversations, I'm sure. The food's good, just dinners for me, when I can get there on time. But they'll make me a plate so I can eat later. Danier's a really busy mortuary. Think I'll have some 24/7's."

Owen touched her shoulder, "From death to a quick placement in a casket."

"Right, most families in this area want a casket funeral, with a burial soon after, in whatever location the family chooses. So, on so many fronts, we have to act, and act fast. Families, I'm finding, want a quick resolution."

"So, Mandy, they can get on with their lives."

"Uh huh, the grieving process takes a lot of time; our families face that."

"These families, sounds like you treat each, like your mom, or your dad, or other family members."

"We have to; we are caretakers of the grieving."

"Remember, years ago, when I first started seeing you, I told you that you have a calling."

"Right, we stand shoulder to shoulder with the minister, the coroner or medical examiner, all who work with the dead and their families; it is definitely a calling."

"Then on Friday nights you'll drive to Ankmer?"

"I will, still got my volunteer work on the Saturdays I'm not tied up with the mortuary. And remember, I'll only be at the practicum for eight weeks; the rest of the semester I'll be back at cc finishing up my coursework. I gotta take my National Board Exam for my field, and then I must get registered with Iowa State Board of Mortuary Science."

"You can't practice 'til that's all done."

"Right."

"May not say it later, so'll say it now, Mandy, I'll be with you, in my prayers and thoughts, every step of the way through your practicum and return to campus. I know you have to study for the National Boards."

"Uh huh, I already bought the exam books for studying; it'll be every second I'm not working at Danier, nights, and nights back on campus, along with studying for all my classes."

"So I'll stay back here, in our home, finishing it up, and I'll not come to see you until you let me know. It's too much stuff to try to balance out; you must have time to study, finals, boards."

Mandy began to cry as she buried her face in his shoulder.

"Oh Owen, thank you for understanding; you're already my wonderful partner, in this whole effort."

He held her as he heard her say, "These are tears of relief, knowing that you understand, that you're by my side, in your mind."

"Sweetheart, I just had no idea how intense the end of your program would be."

She moved from him and wiped her eyes. She looked up into his eyes, "Honestly, I didn't realize it either, until now, so entrenched in the program, so close to finishing up."

They lightened the mood, fixing pumpkin pie with dollops of whipped cream on top, and more coffee, getting dessert for her parents and joining them for the end of the football game. After that they took their homework and sat on the floor next to each other in Mandy's bedroom.

They handed each other the one page to explain who each was, their values, beliefs, future plans. They read each other's stories out loud. Together they read through the pages of their own explanations about finances, religious beliefs, and future family.

"Unbelievable, Owen, our whole future lives, kinda laid out on paper."

"Sure important, I think, at least I'm ready for our talk with reverend before the wedding. We've known each other a little bit for a long time, but this is the deep, gut-stuff that'll help get us through some rough times, that all couples go through, to make this work for us. I've learned so much about you, in this discussion we've had the last hour."

"And I've learned a lot about you, we're actually kinda blank slates to each other," Mandy smiled to Owen and touched his cheek.

He took her hand and kissed it.

"This's kinda scary stuff."

"Like, the whole rest of our lives, the romance is just one piece of the relationship we're gonna have, Owen."

They got up and stretched. Together they walked back into the great room where her folks sat in front of the fire.

"How'd it go, the prenuptial work?"

"So much to learn still, about each other."

"Kids," Jim spoke up as Owen and Mandy stood near them, "the rest of your lives, this'll go on." He patted Cindy's hand, "And just when you think you've got your gal figured out, she'll do something, well different."

"So it's true what guys say, "Uh, she's just a mystery to me.""

They all laughed together, as Jim nodded, "Hey, that's for sure."

℘

Mandy listened to her voice mail after she got home from the campus library. Her rule became to turn her phone off, to let messages go to voice mail. The process worked for her, now for three semesters. She listened to Owen, his voice hoarse.

"Sweetheart, I got a bad something; I'm taking stuff, gotta get well. We're getting married, hooray."

She heard the weakness of his voice. As she continued to listen the tears started and her nose drained. When she hung up, she cried for several minutes. Mandy got up from her spot on the floor and washed her face at the bathroom sink. She applied moisturizer and talked to her mirror.

"So, Owen deploys on the 28th. We marry on the 26th. He says it'll be two weeks, probably not longer, 'cause he's already done his two week mandatory commitment for this year. Remember, doofus, so long ago he told me, we talked about it, that deployments were always possible, that Air National Guard went when and where they were told. That's at least four more years, Mandy, get used to it. It's his military service, what he wants to do, cause there's still trouble in lots of places."

She forced herself to smile into the mirror and then she walked back into her bedroom for several more hours of studying. After an hour she went to the kitchen to make herself two cups of coffee. Her other roommate for this term did not drink coffee. After it perked she drank the coffee, starting to feel better about the short time she and Owen would share after their wedding.

She returned to her room with the second cup, sat on the floor, and prayed out, "Thank you God for my life, and You'll help us decide on a honeymoon."

Mandy felt a blanket-like warmth cover her for the rest of her study time that night.

5

Christmas 2012

"Happy?"

"Oh, Owen, yes, and I love you so. Isn't this fun, having these folks around us, celebrating us?" she smiled up to her husband.

"Yes, fun, you are so beautiful. The light in your brown eyes, so intense."

They cut the cake early, getting several pictures of them feeding each other. Because Mandy liked chocolate and Owen liked carrot cake, the cake had two layers, side by side, instead of on top of each other. That way each guest could pick their kind of cake, or a little of each. Another sheet cake sat nearby, if needed. The couple's plan remained to freeze what was left, for a cake and ice cream celebration when Mandy finished her program in May.

They mingled with the folks who came to their come-and-go reception, having cake, champagne punch, and little finger sandwiches. Memaw, Granddad Overton, and Cindy's folks enjoyed meeting the guests.

"A joyous occasion," Granddad Overton shared with the three of them, "such an awesome Christmas present, us getting a son, and memaw, getting a daughter."

A guitar appeared via Tom and the sound of John Denver's "Annie's Song" could be heard along with other love songs.

"We didn't know you played," Mandy smiled to Tom Hoskisson.

"Oh, yes, even for a funeral or two."

"Thank you, Tom and thanks to you and Kristy for coming. I'm so looking forward to applying to work for you in a few months."

"Not as much as we are; we keep getting busier, still the only home in town."

They thanked each guest for coming just this day after Christmas, before they departed. Owen shared his deployment on the 28th, and Mandy let folks know about her funeral services practicum and final coursework. The last guests left, wishing them a happy and blessed life.

"You two," the caterers announced, "throw another log on that Yule fire; we'll finish cleaning up and get out of here. We heard you've only got a couple nights together before Owen deploys."

"Thanks," Owen smiled to them.

They sat in front of the wood fire and Amy, caterer in charge, brought them cake and champagne punch before the caterers left. Soon all they heard were the hissing and sparking sounds of the fire as it started to diminish.

"I love you, Owen."

He took her hand after they finished their cake, "And I love you, Mandy. Your dress, so pretty, you never told me the dress details, how you got it."

"Yup, I got to play dress up at gran's. She kept old outfits for Sally Ann and me to dress up in. In the back of another bedroom closet there was a long dress with a cloth covering. Underneath were two layers of plastic, and under that, gran's wedding dress. She showed me the dress on one of the last days I stayed with her after school, back when either dad or mom picked me up. And she asked me to try it on. For sure, as I grew, it seemed a possibility of a wedding dress for me."

"And here it is, did ya feel like gran, like she was right here?"

"I for sure did, for this day. And gran, I'm sure was watching, the seamstress and me, figuring out how to add sleeves to a sleeveless dress, what material to use to make the dress pretty. She and granddad married in late summer. So I needed to make the dress work for Christmas, none of that showing bare arms."

"Yeah, your clothes now, dark grays, blues, blacks, somber, serious."

"Yup, you understand completely, the role I'll be playing."

"So it was nice you got to wear."

She added, "Something to match our Christmas cheer."

"It was a simple, beautiful ceremony."

"The best, intimate, just our families."

They kissed and kissed. And then they held each other tight.

"For all the nights we can't be together for the next few months."

"Mandy, so exciting, unexpected, our coming together for the first time, at your place in Ankmer."

"But Owen, I bled a lot, not sure why, 'cause you were so gentle with me."

"So are you healing, no more bleeding, or soreness?"

"Yeah, I think I'm all healed. I want you."

"And I want you."

Owen left the embers burning in the fireplace and put on a Christmas CD. They danced their way to the bedroom, Mandy and Owen's bedroom.

"My first time in your bedroom, in your bed."

He held her close as the music continued.

"This is our bedroom, our bed," he emphasized, as he bent and kissed her.

They took their time undressing each other. He helped her lay her wedding dress on the floor away from them. They rubbed each other's backs and buttocks, kissing and caressing as their hands moved down each other's bodies. He picked her up and lay her on their bed. She reached up and pulled him down to her.

"My wonderful husband."

"And my wonderful wife."

He felt the throbbing in his penis intensify as he gently eased into her hot slickness. They thrust together again and again and climaxed, whispering each other's names.

"Your gift to me, Owen."

He nestled his head next to hers. And in a little while he lifted himself from her. They came together, facing each other on their sides.

"You are my precious, precious one, Mandy."

"I love making love with you."

"Kinda what you expected?"

"Not, well, the first time, no."

"But now?"

"I want to make love with you, again, now."

She moved on top of him, sat up and began covering his face and neck with kisses. As she eased down and into him, "Together, now, and when our hair's silver, we'll be, like this."

"I told you once, when I showed you the land where this home would be, that you were my light, your smile, to wake up to every morning."

They thrust together in slow strokes, feeling their tension building, faster and faster. He gave his seed to her as she climaxed with him. After a little while Mandy moved from him as the afterglow of their lovemaking subsided.

They wrapped in each other's arms and drifted off. Several hours later Owen awoke to see Mandy looking into his eyes.

"Like having a bed buddy?"

Mandy laughed and laughed, catching Owen up in her glee, "Yeah, sweetheart, I super enjoy having a bed buddy. It'll take some getting used to."

"But we're gonna be apart so much."

"Come the summer, Mandy, then it'll finally happen, the every day bed buddy part."

"It's gonna be so wunerful," she kissed him smack on the lips.

"Hungry?"

"Starved, let's hop up, fix the fire back up, with the Christmas music, and we can have finger sandwiches, more cake, and more punch, what'cha say."

"Always you get to my heart, through my tummy."

They sat on the hardwood floor, with a soft area rug under them, and ate more of their reception food as they stared into the bristling fire. After they cleaned up, they returned to the rug and lay next to each other on the floor, wrapping up in a comforter. Owen woke to the dark of the home, except for the dying fire. He picked sleeping Mandy up and carried her to their bedroom.

The morning sun blanketed the bed as they awoke.

"Hello, Mrs. Northwood."

Mandy crossed her eyes to him and stuck her tongue to the left outside her mouth, "Uh, who's that?"

They laughed together.

"Uh huh, I'll get my name changed at school, and at so many other places in the next few weeks. First thing, I gotta fix us a big breakfast. We have just this next 24 hours together."

They helped each other fix the meal. Owen downed several eggs, six pieces of bacon, and three pieces of toast. Mandy ate less than that.

"Goodness, I guess I'll learn how much you can eat."

"That's lots, my dear girl."

They dressed together back in their bedroom, sweatshirts and blue jeans for the day. Then they tackled the wedding presents set on the dining room table. Their reception guests all knew they needed several pieces of furniture, so a money tree yielded enough for them to purchase a sectional couch they had picked out for in front of the fireplace. Mandy kept track of the names of the gift givers. She had all guest addresses, so made it her job to send thank you notes immediately, as soon as Owen departed.

"Time, dear wife, to show you how your home operates, in case, you're out here by yourself, at some point. I've written down instructions, in this trusty notebook, for just in case."

He showed her the notebook location at a bottom kitchen shelf.   He spoke out what he wrote as he gave her a tour of their home.   First they went to the inside of the two-car garage. He showed her the electrical box, how to turn off power to the home, and the detailed circuit breakers, marked as to where they were located in the home. They headed for the basement.

"It's been drywalled and primer painted. We just gotta figure out what colors you might want, and the kind of flooring over the concrete."

"It looks as if you've planned a big, like man cave, a bedroom, with a bathroom with a shower, and a laundry room that also holds the furnace and water heater."

He spent time explaining how to turn off the water for the home.

"And the furnace is forced air, also Mandy, we have air conditioning. I'll show you the thermostat, up in the hallway on the first floor."

"Yeah, I remember seeing the outside unit for the ac."

She touched the washer and dryer and turned to him, smiling

"These are new, the washer and dryer, oh Owen, how?"

"Mom and Dad, their wedding gift to us."

"Nice, oh my gosh."

"And your folks, Mandy, you didn't know this until now, the nice refrigerator," he paused, "they got that for us."

Mandy felt salty tears forming.

"My folks, I didn't ask for anything, I'm glad they checked in with you."

He came to Mandy and gave her a comforting hug.

"Sometimes, Mandy, I think your folks like me better than they like you."

"I'm sure that's true, 'cause I butt heads with them, not so much as I used to. Do you think they'll ever get used to what I'm gonna be doing?"

"They might not; lots of folks are scared about death and stuff that goes with that. But, they seem to be more accepting, as time goes by, of what is going on with you. My gosh, you're going into the internship, like next week."

She followed him up the steps.

"I for sure gotta add our parents' names to our thank you list."

"I knew you'd take care of that for me."

He showed her the two empty bedrooms with their access to a bathroom.

"These two rooms been primer painted. Pick colors and I'll paint. But I'd like to keep our bedroom that off white, if it's OK with you."

"Of course, you've done so much work on our home; I feel pretty helpless, you going this alone."

"Sweetheart, I've had lots of help. That's just unseen by you. But it hasn't been alone."

"I can't wait to help out, soon as I'm done."

"Darlin," he drawled out in his fake accent, "you best just help them folks out at your new place, I'll take care of this all."

They stood in the hallway together as Mandy burst out laughing, "Oh Owen, I love you so, only you have that accent."

"Yep," he replied.

ॐ

"Another cup of coffee?"

"Thanks."

"Owen, you'll decide," she stopped talking and poured him a cup, " where all our new stuff goes."

"Right, I got the time."

They made order in their bedroom. Mandy hung up her wedding dress, and they decided whose belongings would go where in the closet.

"I'm not bringing a lot of stuff here; I just don't own that many clothes."

"Are we clearing the few things from your closet at home and bringing them here?"

"Uh huh, I want to, that way dad and mom can do whatever they want with my bedroom. I think they need to put a double bed in there for company."

"Sounds like a good idea, what about Michael's room?"

"Yeah, it's already a bedroom for company; someday Michael may come home, along with my mom's folks, so two bedrooms are pretty necessary."

"Did you tell me that you have a double bed frame that we could have?"

"Yeah, my folks saved that from gran's home."

"So one day we can put mattress and bedsprings on it for a guest room, one of our bedrooms."

"Right, Owen, you're thinkin' way ahead of me, thank you for that. 'Bout all I can do is put one foot in front of the other, until I get to Des Moines, and been in my internship for a few days."

He held her tight as they stood in their sunlit bedroom.

"Let's get to town, and get back here, I have a special dinner planned for us."

"You do, wow, that's wunerful," he kissed her on top of her head as they stood back from each other.

She looked out the window at the snow-covered ground. She took his hand and looked up into his eyes.

"Been meaning to share with you, since you'll be gone for a little while, and me, longer. God, He's with us, beside us, in all our hours. And Owen, I believe, with all my heart, and based on what I know so far, that I will go home to God one day. This is my home for right now," she shook her head, "but I'm not really home."

He continued to gaze into her eyes, "And that is what I believe, that this world we know now, it's just a preparation for our real home, with God, one day."

"I welcome that day."

"As do I, Mandy."

On the trip to town to get her final possessions from her parents' home Mandy asked.

"What about those snowy winter days, or nights for me sometimes, how'm I gonna get out of our lane and onto the paved county road?"

"Got it covered, dad's got a snow plow on the front of an old jeep we use for the heavier snows. When it looks like I'll need it to get you to work, I'll drive it over from dad's, plow him a patch out to the road, plow us out and then finish plowing him out."

"Whew, you think of everything. And you'll teach me how to use the equipment, if I need to."

"I do," he paused and gave her a wink, "think of everything my dear and yes, I'll teach you how to do the snowplowing," he patted her knee and smiled to her.

"Can't help it, I love you so much, Owen, you care, even about my driving in the Iowa snow."

They hugged as soon as they got out of the vehicle.

∞

"You ready for this?"

"Yes," Mandy nodded her head to Justin Danier. "I'm in my frame of mind to help this family. It's been a heartbreaking time for them."

"So, you do understand, you've mentioned you experienced so much in your hometown mortuary work."

"I did see so much, but only one child."

"I'm making you lead for this at-need family. I know you met with the father and his sister, when they first came in, two days before Jordy's death this morning."

"We'll take care of this family, Justin. Ben and I are headed to pick up the body and take care of the embalming process. The casket the father wants is on site, so they need to bring in the outfit they want Jordy to be buried in. He said he'd have that to us by this afternoon."

"And the service and reception, is that getting planned out?"

"Correct, it's nice that both the service and reception'll be done right here at the mortuary. The mom's got the service planned out with the reverend. And the reception with catering, she's planning that also."

"How many're we expecting?"

"She thinks 140 people max, which is just 25 short of our capacity for both the ceremony room and the reception room. So that'll work out nicely."

ဢ

They hugged each other as they cried. It took several minutes for them to settle down. They gazed at each other as they shook their heads.

Ben blew out a big breath, "Our first embalming experience, on our own. You did great, Mandy, the tiny bit of makeup and his hair's so short, didn't do anything else."

"And so did you, Ben, did great."

They stood next to each other, then turned and looked at Jordy.

"What a beautiful young man; the casket will only be open for the family to view before the ceremony. Then we'll close it up."

Together they dressed Jordy in a handsome suit his mom said he only wore once, before his blinding-fast brain tumor appeared. Late that afternoon Mandy got a call, before she headed for her rooming house.

"I need your help, Mandy."

"Of course, what can I do?"

"Chuckie, he was a friend to Jordy. They were in different classes, but they had orchestra together."

"OK, how can we help?"

"Uh, the back story, Chuckie and Jordy met in 4th grade orchestra, two years ago. They both play violin. Oh how they loved playing; they both took lessons and got pretty good at the instrument. Anyway, I got a phone call from Chuckie's mom. She told me how devastated he was about Jordy's death. That tumor took him so quick; it caught all the kids by surprise."

Sylvia Chapman paused, as Mandy heard her voice begin to choke.

"Chuckie and his pals in the orchestra, they want to play a final tribute to Jordy."

Mandy's mind raced ahead, "What about at the reception?"

"That would be so wonderful; would there be room to have 18 students come to the reception, and do their tribute to Jordy there?"

"I'm certain; only thing, they'd have to bring their own stands for their music, or play from memory. We'd provide the chairs, of course. How wonderful, Sylvia, I'm helping with everything connected with Jordy."

"That'll mean, you'll put the refreshment table in a different location from what we discussed?"

"Exactly, we'll make certain that Chuckie and his orchestra are front and center at the reception. And that they perform when they want to."

"Is that OK with you, let the young people decide?"

"Yes, they'll decide, I just need to step back and let you all do your work."

"Thank you for that, Sylvia."

"And the burial, is that planned out?"

"Right, my fellow home helper and I deliver Jordy to you and your family at the Chapman family site in Doncaster. It's an hour away, and it's at 10 a.m. the day after Jordy's celebration here in Porttown. And we'll have the cemetery helpers finish up after you have your private together time with Jordy. You're planning a family luncheon in Doncaster. We'll take care of everything else."

"Good, and the funeral flowers, if there are any?"

"As you indicated, when Ben and I return from Doncaster, we'll fix bouquets from the ceremony and deliver them to folks at the hospital you've designated in Des Moines. It's wonderful that you want the sick to enjoy Jordy's flowers."

"That's it, Mandy, I think we've got it settled. Chuckie's mom, Olivia, plans to come to the mortuary tomorrow to see about the orchestra setup."

"I'll be here for her; I'll see you all the next morning at 10:30 for his celebration."

"See you then, and you've been wonderful, so young to have your gentle understanding, your empathy for our grief, our devastation."

"Thank you; we're here to assist you."

℘

Olivia Hapshear shook Mandy's hand as they met at Danier's the next morning.

"Thank you for seeing me. I'm just shaken to my core, losing a child, it's got to be the most devastating situation a parent can go through."

Mandy took her to the reception area. She had it set up with 7 round tables on each side of the room with 10 chairs at each table, a little crowded but it was her thought for now.

"So, I want Chuckie and his 17 other musicians to be front and center for all of this. The reception table's along the back."

Olivia walked around inside the reception room.

"Yes, I can see that this will work out. The musicians' chairs are all set up. Chuckie will just stand to start the music off, then they'll all play. You'll be surprised at the musical talent they all possess. I think there's a possibility that their orchestra teacher will be able to get away to watch his students perform."

"And they're all fifth and sixth graders?"

"That's right; some've been together now for two years."

℘

"Am I ready?" she asked herself as she picked up her bag for the day at Danier's.

"Today, Jordy, this is your next to last day with your family," she paused, "at least on this earth."

Her mind whirled back on her short acquaintance with the young man whose funeral she would manage in a little while. He had bold blue eyes and short, very short reddish hair. It just started to grow back from the surgery to remove the tumor. The docs thought they got it all, but God had a different idea. "Jordy, you're watching with God and his angels, seeing your folks, I'm certain," she spoke out as she walked the blocks from her rooming house to the mortuary.

An hour later she felt ready to support the Chapman family as they celebrated Jordy. She met with the chaplain and the organist and got their go ahead for the programs that Jordy's mom wanted for the funeral. The caterers brought the sandwiches, drinks, glassware, plastic plates and silverware and two different kinds of cake for the reception. They put on bright red tablecloths and bright blue paper napkins and set the tables seating 10 at a table. Jordy's mom mentioned his favorite colors always were red and blue.

Outside in the hall a blown up picture of Jordy stood on a tripod. Mandy touched the side of the picture, seeing Jordy in his blue soccer uniform with the name, Maxim Force, a huge smile on his face.

"Hey, Jordy, great pic," Mandy whispered. Then she looked up, thinking for a second of her gran. "This one, this time, this's for you, Jordy."

The celebration service lasted 15 minutes. Folks mingled in the chapel area, out in the hall and through the entire reception area. The orchestra set up their instruments. Mandy met Chuckie.

"No music stands, Chuckie?"

"No, we have two songs memorized; never know when or where we might have a chance to play, so we're ready to go when everyone comes in and stands or is seated.

"Just asking, but there's an empty chair in the first orchestra row."

"Yeah, that's Jordy's chair.

"An empty chair?" Mandy repeated the words. Chuckie heard the questioning in her voice.

"That's right, I'm gonna talk to everyone about Jordy and the empty chair."

After the short celebration the family asked that everyone come into the reception area for the special music. Some guests found seats at the round tables, and a number stood.

The orchestra gathered and tuned their violins in the large middle area between the chapel and the reception area. They filed in and took their places, facing Jordy's guests.

The family asked Mandy to introduce Chuckie and the orchestra as a large group. Later the orchestra members would come around and sit with guests. She made the introductions and Chuckie began. He pointed to the empty chair right behind him. His own seat was right next to that one.

"Empty Chair," he said as he looked around and then down to the empty chair. He looked up and began.

"You're my special friend. When we got teased for playing the violin, we just blew it off. We're also athletes, soccer players, like your picture out in the hall shows. We're the Maxim Force. So Jordy, we got this chair set up for you, right here. All of us in the orchestra," he paused and looked around, nodding, "we know you're here, your spirit, your music. I'll be able to hear you playing, right along with me and the rest of us, that isn't gonna change.

So it's your strength, in spite of what you knew might happen, that's made me appreciate you, Jordy. My whiny days are over, a scrape or a sprain, hey, that's nuthin' compared to what happened to your head. So, for me, like all the kids here who're gonna play for you, it's what's goin' on right now, that's it. Right now, present time, we all gotta enjoy this time, 'cause tomorrow, we don't know what's gonna happen to us. Hey, I sure know that you're standing straight and strong, with God, and that, yeah, you're certainly with us right now. So here's the first song, one we all composed together, when you couldn't come to orchestra practice any more. We call it "Ode to Jordy."

Chuckie turned to his group, brought them to attention. With his nod they began playing the piece. He sat down about half way through the song and stayed seated, playing with his group until the end.

Mandy stood to the side with other guests, listening to the lovely lilt of the piece. She felt quiet tears slid down her cheeks.

"Oh my gosh," she wiped her face as she thought, "I'm so overcome I can't hardly swallow."

She looked around. Outside of the orchestra, everyone in the assemblage had tears.

For moments after the orchestra finished, the entire area remained silent. Then Mandy heard an onslaught of clapping and cheers. Once they quieted, Chuckie stood and shared.

"Jordy loved to play fun stuff, and well, dude," he paused, "we enjoyed the music he came up with. So, "Puff the Magic Dragon" was a child's song he sang and played on his violin. It became our warmup piece before we practiced."

Mandy watched Chuckie look up and smile.

"Yeah, he's smiling to Jordy, like I smiled to gran," she whispered.

He stood and with his nod the orchestra played the song. Guests who remembered the song from childhood sang along. When they finished, the orchestra stood up and began clapping. Soon, they chanted "Jordy, Jordy, Jordy,"

The whole group who were seated around the tables stood and joined the chant. Mandy moved back toward the caterers who waited in the hall. She signaled them that it was time for food and folks enjoying each other. Mandy spent the next few minutes making certain she thanked each musician for his or her part. The music added such a vibrancy to the occasion.

"They're so young, so beautiful and talented. Young people, they are our hope, our future."

Mandy heard that from many of the people with whom she exchanged greetings after the music and as the assemblage got their desserts. She got to meet the orchestra music teacher.

"You must be Mandy."

They shook hands as Mandy nodded to him.

"Sylvia told me that you were the person suggesting that the orchestra play right here in the reception area, so all the guests could hear my talented students."

"Right, I have complete charge of everything for Jordy. He's going to be buried in Doncaster tomorrow, so that and the distribution of his flowers will be most of the last tasks I'll have for him."

"We'll all really miss Jordy. But today was quite a celebration for him. That Chuckie, he's some young man."

"Uh huh, and from what Jordy's mom, Sylvia, said, your whole group of musicians, they're quite special."

"I've tried to instill discipline, respect, and also a love of music in all of them."

"Keep up the wonderful work, David."

"I'll sure try; it'll be tough to replace Jordy."

"Time, it'll take time."

"Thank you again for your insight, letting folks see a bit of Jordy's world."

"It's been my pleasure."

℘

As she walked home from the very full day at the mortuary, her mind circled again and again through the events for Jordy.

"Dare I even ask how your day went?" Joe, a statehouse intern, asked.

"Funeral and reception for a young man, brain tumor took him to God."

She turned and looked to Joe as they sat at the dining room table in her rooming house.

"Think you'll get used to all the emotion involved with the families you help?"

"Not sure, this is my first one where I got to do most of the work. Course, a supervisor looks out for me, just in case. And tomorrow morning we transport the young man to his gravesite; he'll be buried in Doncaster."

"Hey, good luck with the rest of your process; no way I could ever do that kinda work. It takes a special person, to understand all the emotion."

"Right, you are correct that there's lots of emotion, and thanks for the good luck. I think my fellow mortuary intern and I, well, we'll be OK."

She decided she was too emotional to even leave a message for Owen. He was still on deployment, with an end date unknown. Mandy tossed and turned that night. She awoke with a start at 4 a.m., got down on her knees and prayed that she would get through the coming morning.

"Easier, Ben and I, just do the delivery, and get back to Danier's to figure out what to do with the flowers. That'll be fun."

She repeated that twice as she got up from her kneeling and started her small coffee pot. She kept it in her room for just such early days.

"If you drive over, I'll drive back," Ben mentioned after they placed Jordy in the van for the transport to Doncaster. Mandy watched the skies as she drove into the Doncaster graveyard. She heard a forecast for flurries later in the day. With their instructions they found the open grave. The family wanted to be there to greet Jordy and walk along side him as his casket got transported to the grave.

Mandy and Ben stood back away from the family activity. As the family retreated back to their cars, Sylvia came to them and expressed her thanks, and again, for helping to get the flowers to the hospital. Once the grave helpers began to lower the casket, they waved to Mandy and Ben that it was OK for them to head back to Des Moines. Jordy's family decided that it was too much heartache to watch his casket being lowered. That's why they left directly after the gathering. It amazed Mandy how different families handled all the proceedings for their beloved departed one.

They were silent in the van, as Ben drove them back to Des Moines. They listened to favorite songs from CD's they brought for the ride. *Cold Play* and *The Backstreet Boys* were two groups they both liked.

Before they headed to the funeral area, they checked in on the paperwork, especially the financial papers for the Chapman family. Mandy wanted Ben to check her work, especially the math, to make certain everything was in order. He agreed with her figures, so that they could pass the paperwork on to the supervisor for approval.

"Think all of this'll get a little easier, Mandy?"

"Dunno, each situation is different, we must roll with it, one day at a time. This sure as heck is not like an office job with regular hours."

"Yeah, like our last task is to fix up flowers for Memorial. Bet we never do that again."

"But isn't it nice that the family wants sick folks to enjoy the flowers?"

"For sure."

They spent the next two hours fixing flowers in an array of vases that Danier stored for just such situations. Then they transported eight red and white bouquets of flowers. When they checked in with the hospital front desk, there was a cart for the bouquets. And the patients already were assigned the flowers.

"What a sense of relief," Mandy blew out a breath as she turned to Ben, "knowing a healing person is getting that brightness for their hospital room."

"Did you hear what the volunteer told me?"

"Nope."

"She said that the flowers were headed to folks who could enjoy looking at them, and these were folks who had few visitors."

"Sheez, that's so great, Ben."

"Yeah, flowers, they're a wonderful companion to healing."

Owen left her a voice mail, that his deployment would go on for two more weeks. It would take that long to help clean up from the flooding after the huge snowstorm and then the sudden warm up, in that Midwestern town.

₧

During the next week Mandy helped in the business office, learning how Danier handled operatives, merchandising, and home management. They managed quite a bit different from what she learned in her classes. But she remembered what her instructors emphasized, that every funeral business had their own way of handling the death process. That weekend she drove back to Ankmer early Saturday morning in time to work her shift at the ER.

"I'm glad to be back here," she told a nurse on duty, "I'm in my funeral services practicum, so much stuff to learn, surrounding death."

"Yeah, here you get to at least see some healing, folks getting better, getting back to some part of better health than they had before."

Mandy looked Malc in the eye, "It's the finality, not sure I'll ever get used to that. But helping families cope with their grief, that's what gets me through the event."

"You'll be there at that mortuary, how many more weeks?"

"Four, done four and four to go."

"So, you're getting a taste for what goes on."

"I am, Malc, a lot of fear, I'm amazed at how fearful folks are of death. Gotta head out, I got beds to make in the dirty rooms."

"See ya," he replied.

Mandy looked at the big screen with its spreadsheet, indicating clean and dirty rooms.

After she left the ER at her shift's end, she decided to visit the hospital chapel. It was small, just big enough for up to 10 people, but it felt cozy.

"God, You're here, I can really feel You in this nice warm room."

Mandy sat in the upholstered chair, closed her eyes, and put her hands together. She let her mind drift over the past weeks at Danier. She knew one thing for certain, she had a super huge number of things to learn. The deeper into the funeral service practicum she got, the more she realized what a newbee she really was.

She mused, then spoke out, "It was so easy in high school, the coming and going, but I had no idea what really went on at the mortuary."

Mandy opened her eyes, "Thank you, God," she whispered.

She got up, gathered her gear, and headed for the apartment. She studied for the rest of that afternoon and into the night for her National Board. Mandy took time the next morning to attend church and later to run. That night she returned to Des Moines, working on the journal she kept of every activity she participated in at Danier's.

When she arrived at her desk at Danier's on Tuesday after lunch, she found a vase of 12 red roses. She read the card, "Counting the hours, 'til you're in my arms again. Love, Owen."

That night she left him a voice mail of thanks. When she didn't hear from him, she knew he was out on some duty, helping folks.

ɛͻ

On Wednesday of the seventh week of her practicum she and Ben partnered for the fifth time on a funeral.

"Oh Ben, she reminds me so much of my gran, the blonde hair, and her pleasant face. I bet she had a great smile."

"Yeah, my grandma, I lost her a few years back. She was older, but nice, loved me, doted on me, said I would do special things in my life."

"I think she meant what you're doing right now, special."

"Maybe, you might be right about that."

"Well, my gran, just had me and my older brother."

They prepared the body for a public viewing that would take place in the chapel area of the mortuary that afternoon. This time there would be two more aspects to the affair for this woman the next day. The family planned a funeral service at Danier's, with a reception immediately after in the reception area. The deceased's husband gave Mandy a copy of what the service would contain, no minister, just several folks to speak. He also planned the reception for the rest of the family.

"No alcohol, Mandy?"

She noted his unhappy demeanor, and irritating tone, "I'm sorry, but we do not have an alcohol license. Perhaps you folks would want to gather later at a location that allows that."

"Yeah, we'll have to do that; I'll sure as hell need a drink by then."

Mandy stopped herself from making a comment in her mind, or out loud. She tried to remember all the different ways grief masked itself, especially early on after a family member died.

The next day, she stood back, as the person in charge, for the funeral and reception. A young girl spoke at the funeral, and it brought Mandy to tears.

"She reminds me of me, at 14, at gran's funeral. That girl's hurtin' real bad, just like I did. "

Tears came to Mandy's eyes. She felt sad, her spirits down, as she helped the caterers prepare the room for the reception. It turned out to be a quiet affair, not like gran's with all the students there. Just a few young people, she guessed, family members attended. She saw mostly people the age of the husband. Guests finished their food, made their condolences to the family, and left. Soon the daughter of the deceased found her dad. They came to Mandy and thanked her. Once again, she and Ben took the casket to the prepared grave in the designated Des Moines graveyard. No one came to the grave except the funeral grave workers.

"You're really quiet, Mandy."

"Uh huh, thinkin' of my gran, of the wonderful reception we had for her. I miss her, right now, just so much."

"I miss my grandma; this kinda stuff really brings it all back."

They pulled into the van's parking place in the back of the mortuary. Several other cars, some from the reception, still parked there. Mandy began to sob as soon as she got out of the van.

"I'm so sorry, Mandy, your gran, she musta been super special."

Mandy looked at him and nodded, "She was."

They hugged for a time and said together, "One day at a time."

He kissed her forehead and let go of her, "Ready to go in?"

6

Spring 2013

Owen waited and waited, just about ready to leave the parking lot. Earlier Danier informed him that Mandy and Ben would be returning most any time. He got out of his car as he saw a white van pull into the area where he suspected bodies came in and out.

He watched as Mandy and a young man in a black suit got out of the van and hugged. He watched as they talked to each other. Mandy took a step away from him. Owen watched him touch her shoulder and kiss her on her forehead. He watched her nod to the young man and wipe tears from her face. They walked close together into the personnel entrance, holding hands.

Anger blanketed Owen's mind as he continued to stand there.

"Mandy," he whispered, "you're a married woman, what the heck are you doing with this guy? I saw her tears; I gotta talk to her." He took some deep breaths and let them out slow. "Settle down, Owen 'cause you don't know the story, you're assuming stupid stuff."

He came to Des Moines to surprise Mandy; they had not been together since the day after they married. His deployment ran over; the corn crop was near ready for planting. And Mandy kept so busy with her internship, she couldn't get time away, even on the weekend. Since they couldn't jive their schedules, as soon as Owen saw a chance at the farm, he drove to the mortuary in Des Moines.

Owen smiled to the receptionist and introduced himself. She asked him to be seated and went to look for Mandy. He got concerned because 11 minutes passed. She strode toward him as he stood up.

"God blesses us, Owen it's so good to see you."

They hugged. She lifted her face to him and gave him a soft kiss. They hugged again, and Mandy led him to the outer family area. They sat next to each other on a large comfortable couch. She took his hand.

"I'm in my at-need family situation, so I have to get back to help with planning. The family is here; the death occurred yesterday. And they want a fast resolution."

"Wow, I can tell from your voice that you've got a stressful time, Mandy."

"I'll be, well, I'll be better when I can get away today."

"Do you think we can spend a little while together; I can meet you at your rooming house, say at 6?"

She smiled to him, "Think I'll be wrapping the session up by then."

"Once we get food I'll need to head back to Porttown."

"You got stuff, and I do, so that'll work."

ᘒ

They sat across from each other at a hamburger joint near where Mandy lived. The earlier quiet crowd they heard started livening up, with drinks and food in them. Mandy explained the rest of her time at Danier, and then the final four weeks at Ankmer. She shared how much time she spent studying, for Boards coming up and for her coursework, once she got back to school.

"You don't have a life now, Mandy."

"I told you, Owen, but it's not for much longer."

"Mandy, I saw you with that young man, in the black suit, as you two got out of the van and hugged each other. Mandy, he kissed you."

"Yes, he did, trying to comfort me. We'd just buried a woman, who even looked a lot like gran. Together we did the embalming, prep for burial, everything. Interns work on all that stuff, uh, under supervision. He's a fellow intern, in preparation for the day that we'll go it alone, like I'll have to, once I get back to Hoskisson's. Hey, I still gotta apply for the position there, it's not a given. I won't always have a partner to work with."

"I didn't like what I saw," Owen spat out the words.

She looked him in the eye. He looked into her brown eyes, stone cold, her lips thin.

"Ben and I've worked together almost seven weeks; we've felt, seen, and absorbed some pretty terrible stuff, not just about the corpse, but having to do with all the different family dynamics, like the worst in some people comes out when they're grieving. So him and me, we've gotten close, things you and me, well, we can never share, nor can I ever talk about. It's an emotionally charged scenario, and each death is so different. So yeah, there's an intimacy between Ben and me, that just is there, can't be helped. We've talked each other down from some pretty terrible scenes, OD, suicide."

"Are you sure you want to do this kind of work?"

She nodded to him, a smile on her face, "Always and forever, it's what I'm meant to do. I pray a lot. And it's never been more clear to me, in watching death, that God's right beside me, guiding me, sometimes picking me up and shoving me along when things get rough."

"I don't like what I saw, you and Ben. I hate to say this, but I felt super jealous, of him being there, kissing your forehead, instead of me."

Mandy's felt her face flare beet red.

"I'm doing the best I can; Owen, it's just a few more days, and then I'm back at Ankmer. I consider this training an opportunity God's given me. Please give me time; you now see what happens, can happen, in emotionally charged situations. He was comforting me; I was crying. The dead woman, so much like gran. I've hugged him many times, when we've both broken down; the grief does not escape us; we're caught up in it, like a whirlwind, out of control, until time steadies us."

"I'm heading back to Porttown now. I'll drop you at your place. I'm totally upset, mostly with myself. I think I won't call you again, until you get back to the cc. This whole deal is way more than I can deal with now."

"God's in charge, Owen, we'll get this all worked out, thank you for dinner. And I hope the fields'll be ready for planting, just the way you want."

She watched as he did not smile to her, after her message of hope for the planting. He let her off at the rooming house. Mandy only heard silence as she closed the door and waved to him.

Mandy felt anger and sadness, for and with Owen. She doubted now that they should ever have gotten married, so quick and then gone from each other. Could they make it until she finished? For several days she tossed that about in her head. At night, though, she had to study. And that became a real gift from God for her. Mandy did not get a call from Owen during the next days.

ઠ

The business office employees at Danier Mortuary stood with Mandy and Ben as Justin Danier and his team of corpse-care people came into the conference room with cupcakes and pop.

"Thank you Mandy and Ben for your outstanding work these past weeks. We've enjoyed your young vitality and positive attitude. You would not believe how much that helps our grieving families. In you, they see a future, when once again they'll smile, and even laugh a little. We all agree that the young man, Jordy, that his death, and the way you handled the outstanding reception, well, none of us who were here can ever forget all that. You two are the future, a bright future for mortuary science. And Mandy, we're hoping you'll return to your hometown. And Ben, do you have a placement?"

"Two different ones, I'm interviewing. I want to stay in Iowa, for sure."

"How grand, to remain in our state," Polly, the front office receptionist added and began clapping for the two of them.

Everyone clapped as Mandy and Ben gazed around at the group and smiled.

Justin Danier continued to watch over his two interns. Mandy and Ben worked so well together. They were young; she was pretty. And he was a handsome young man. As the last couple days of their internship came, Justin decided he needed to talk to Ben.

They met together, "Don't be concerned Ben, this is not about your work."

He grinned to Justin, "Whew, I didn't know."

The two men gazed at each other.

"I've been watching you and Mandy, and as time's gone on in the internship, well, I don't think I'm mistaking the signs."

Ben nodded his head to his mentor, "Yeah, can't help what I feel. I'm in love with Mandy. And I know, she's just newly married and has had little time with her husband."

"She's talked to you about her husband?"

"She has, so proud of him, in Iowa's Air National Guard, and he's had some difficult deployments. He's also a corn farmer, and he's built a home for the two of them."

"So, Ben, what now, what are you going to do now?"

Ben lifted his teary eyes to Justin.

"What I have to," he nodded, "I have to let her go. I want her to have a successful career and a happy life. She's made it so clear to me that I hafta open my heart to all kinds of love. Hers for me, it's unconditional. Working in this field, with emotions so raw, like wounds, people in such pain, we open our emotions, our hearts to consoling the grieving. She and I agree that's the most important part of what we do, helping the survivors. The rest of it is the business of dealing with the deceased, which seemed so important at first."

"Thank you, Ben, you understand. Go to it, you've got one more funeral coming up."

"I'm looking forward to being the lead for this at-need family. Wow, then I'll be on my own, without you in the background for me to fall back to, Justin."

"Trust me, you'll be fine. Like Mandy, I hope you're studying for your National Board."

"I am, and I still have classes back at my cc, just like Mandy does at hers. Thank you for the talk."

He shook Justin's hand, turned and walked from the office. Ben felt a pain, like a sharp knife stabbing him, right into his heart.

ℰℒ

Mandy mailed her thank you notes to the Danier staff the day before her last day there. She felt salty stinging tears as she went from employee to employee, for a final hug and thanks for all they did to help her with her internship.

She and Ben shared duties on this final funeral for the two of them. At 9 a.m. the family let the mortuary know that the below-freezing temps made it necessary to bring the funeral from the planned one outside in a park to the chapel at Danier.

"This'll be so much better, Ben. We're gonna just roll with this, good lesson for us in the future. The family's gonna speak, and then a friend of the deceased will sing a cappella."

"And we don't have to worry about a reception."

"Yeah, I figure, it's a small group, they'll meet at a restaurant somewhere, after."

"The memorial programs of the deceased?"

Mandy went to the table in the entrance area, "Right here."

"Good, I still get nervous, hoping all goes OK, it's a small presentation and they're taking the ashes, I guess for a future time of burial."

"Ben, I think we always will get nervous, especially stuff that's done here at the mortuary. We don't have much control in a church or outside setting."

Mandy kept drinking coffee through the day; it steadied her, on this emotional last day of her Danier time. At day's end she just wanted to simply leave, to move on to the next segment of her education. She and Ben gathered their gear, Mandy for her walk back to the rooming house, and Ben, for his trip to his school. He got packed and was ready to head out. Mandy wanted to stay one last night. She would head for Ankmer early the next morning.

They walked together out the doors of the mortuary, turned around, and stood there for a time, gazing at the beautiful facility.

"Until we meet again," they shared as they smiled to each other.

Mandy started walking away, to the corner for her trek to her rooming house.

"Mandy, please stop for a moment."

She turned and walked into Ben's arms as he opened his arms to her. They held on to each other for a long time. She loosened her hold on him and stepped back, looking into his eyes.

"I will always love you, Mandy," she heard his choking voice and saw his tears.

Tears shocked her eyes and a huge burning lump paralyzed her throat. She turned and began walking. When she got to the corner, she turned around. Ben was gone.

"I can't believe how I'm reacting to him," she whispered as her tears continued to stream down her cheeks.

"Oh God, I love you, and you love me. You love Ben, and I love Ben. God, bless and keep him. And God, thank you for your blessings to me. Sometimes I forget, but I am grateful, for my life."

∽

"How's the internship?"

"Intense, emotional, grief, it's paralyzing, for families," was her stock answer as she returned to her classes for the last few weeks of the term.

In her first call to Owen that he chose to answer she shared how glad she was to be back in school. Just to study, for her classes, and for the Board, she found that soothing, after the internship. She had time to run. Even working in the ER, it became more a place of hope, than she ever expected.

Mandy took her National Board Exam and applied for her registration with the Iowa State Board of Mortuary Science.

"I'm coming to your ceremony, you finishing up your program, Mandy."

"I'm so glad you've decided to do that."

"You came to my ceremony when I finished my AA in Ag Business."

"I did, but I didn't know what to expect, after everything that's happened."

She heard Owen take a deep breath into the phone, "We're gonna work this all out. Corn's planted; dad's sick."

"Oh Owen," she felt her voice crack as she spoke.

"Yeah, tests now for him, I really am taking over the farm, right now."

"I'm driving to Porttown on Wednesday afternoon, have my interview with the Hoskisson's. You need to know that they're interviewing several other candidates. My getting the job is not a given."

"Mandy, I understand that, for sure, hope it goes well."

"Well, we're all years older. I got a lot more insight, have to see how the mortuary feels about me taking over one day, not sure of their retirement plans."

"I'll see you for your little ceremony."

"Thank you, Owen, all us students in MS, we're so used to receptions and gatherings of every description. None of us want much, just to be together one last time, then to get on with our lives and careers. Some of them still have to take their Boards."

"I love you, Mandy."

"And I love you, Owen."

ℰↄ

He stood and clapped for all the students completing the program.

"I thought there'd be more guys. Mandy mentioned something about a change in the whole mortuary thinking, that more women started to be interested in the program. That's sure the case here."

He watched them as they stood together for pictures, eight women, all dressed in dark suits, mostly black, with white or light blue collared shirts showing above their buttoned suits. The three men in the group wore black suits and subdued dark ties. They seemed as close to being in military attire as any group Owen ever saw. Professional, that was the word he thought of as he gazed at them. Mandy and another woman looked so much alike that Owen took a second glance when he first saw them together in the front of the room. After the short ceremony everyone mingled. Owen found Jim and Cindy Overton as they hugged their daughter.

"Oh my gosh, I wasn't sure whether anyone could make this ceremony. Everyone's got work," Mandy said and gave them her wide smile.

Jim touched his daughter's shoulder, "So much time, such hard work on your part."

They made room for Owen to step in. He hugged Mandy and whispered in her ear, "I'm proud of you."

They kissed and held on to each other.

"We're headed back to Porttown now," they heard Jim's voice.

"I'll stay with Mandy tonight in Ankmer; tomorrow we'll get her moved to our home."

Owen smiled as he emphasized our.

"We'll be in touch, Mom and Dad. Thank you for taking time off to see me finish. I'll let you know what Hoskisson's decides."

"One day at a time, Mandy," her mom touched her shoulder.

"Right."

Mandy felt dizzy, as she got into her car for the drive to her apartment. She knew she had to meet Owen there.

"God, I'm feeling so totally unsure of myself, no job for certain. And starting a new life, I was comfortable at the rooming house and at Ankmer. Lots of change coming for me."

ℂ

"Last night, wonderful, Mandy; I can't believe how much I love you. I don't ever want to be apart from you again, for the long time away at your internship, and school."

"I love you, Owen; don't think we ever knew how hard it would be to be apart like we were."

"For sure, so hard," he said as he held her hand. They sat at the kitchen table having the last coffee Mandy would ever drink in her apartment.

He helped her pack her belongings and finish cleaning up. Mandy was the last person to vacate the apartment. Her other two roommates already left.

"Everything's all cleaned up; want to leave now?"

"Sure, Mandy, whatever's best for you."

They went together to the manager's office to return the apartment key.

Mandy introduced Owen to Celia.

The manager grinned to Mandy, "You're finished, congratulations, it's been quite a journey for you. You gotta be proud," she nodded to Owen.

Mandy handed her the key, "Here, it's really been my home."

Owen followed Mandy to their home outside Porttown. They brought her possessions in and put them in the empty guest bedroom. She fixed them decaf coffee. They sat at the kitchen island to drink it.

"Exhausted?"

"Yeah, Owen, the world's weight seems to be on my shoulders tonight."

"We'll sleep; tomorrow, we got tomorrow."

They spooned together in the bed she only slept in twice. The next morning Mandy heard both the birds chirping and the wind playing in the trees. They made love, slow and then intense, for all the nights they missed each other over the past five months. They slept, then showered. Mandy fixed lots of bacon and toast and eggs. They sat together at the island, chowing down.

"Stuff just tastes better when you cook, Mandy. What is that?"

"You don't like fixing meals, so it's a chore. Food doesn't taste as good when you do yourself."

"That's it, my dear girl, you know some stuff about me, that I can't even figure out myself."

"Remember the old adage, way to man's heart is through the tummy."

"Exactly."

Owen's cell rang. Mandy took the dishes to the sink, rinsed and placed them in the dishwasher. She headed to the bedroom after she watched Owen stand near the living room window, looking out.

She moved to the empty bedroom where they took all her possessions to sort out. She found a shirt and blue jeans to put on, and looked around.

"All this wash to be done, from my school and internship," she spoke out, nodding.

"Mandy, oh Mandy."

Owen stood in the doorway of the bedroom. She turned and came to him. What she heard was distress in his voice.

"What, what, Owen?"

She held out her arms, and he came into a hug.

"Dad, he's fainted again, unconscious for a time. The ambulance took him to Memorial. I gotta head out. Please don't come; I'll call you."

He took her hand and held it until they got into the kitchen.

"Let's sit down; I'll pour us coffee."

"Talk to me, Owen."

"I didn't want to tell you yet, 'cause too much's happened with you lately."

"OK."

"Dad's heart's got problems."

Mandy saw tears form in his eyes. She took a drink of coffee and waited.

"Prognosis, diagnosis, cardiac doc, dad needs an aortic valve replacement."

She nodded to him, catching his eyes, "If he's gonna have any kind of life, like this is the second time he'll be hospitalized for this, right?"

"Right."

"Hey, I'm not the angel of death, but death is my business. Your dad's gotta get help."

"Sheez, Mandy, you're brutal."

"Please call me once the docs get him stabilized."

They stood and hugged.

She whispered to him, "Your mom and dad, I love them very much, lots of times more than I care for my own. You have a way loving family."

He kissed her on top of her head. She watched him move down the drive way in his pickup. She went to the small alcove off the kitchen where they kept the computer and a two-drawer file cabinet. She searched for information on aortic valve replacement. She felt dissatisfied with the first source, so checked a second and third source.

She returned to the kitchen, pouring herself another cup of coffee.

"God, I think Brad'll be OK. But like they diagnosed at the heart place in Des Moines, he needs to get fixed up, like now. This second event," she stopped talking and shook her head.

Owen called her cell two hours later.

"They got him stabilized. He's going to Des Moines; the cardiac doc'll decide on the surgery date."

"Right, after they do all the tests."

"Uh huh, I'm driving mom and dad to the hospital, that's tomorrow, in their sedan. The doc thinks he'll be able to make the ride with us. And I'll stay over one night, I want to donate blood, mom's going to, also. Someone needs it, that's for sure."

"Maybe to replace what your dad," Mandy stopped.

"Might need."

"Exactly, Owen."

"I'll come home for dinner and get ready to go back. Mom's getting gas so we'll be ready to head out early."

ॐ

A few minutes after Owen left to take his parents to the Des Moines hospital Mandy got a call from Hoskisson Mortuary. An hour later she drove to the mortuary, a flood of memories hitting her from the two years she worked there in high school. She parked and stood in front of the complex.

"Changes, there've been changes, to the exterior. I wonder what's happened inside?"

She went in; both the chapel and the reception area seemed larger. But the wonderful sound of running water, from the wall of stone, that had not changed. She noticed that the large living room, that feeling of a comfortable room in a home, remained the same. And she wondered if they still put up the memory Christmas tree for the holidays.

Mandy wore her comfortable black suit with a soft blue shirt. She had four suits for her internship, but this remained her favorite. She stood as Tom Hoskisson strode toward her. She noticed more silver hair as he smiled to her.

"Congratulations, Mandy, you're graduated, passed National Boards. You're still in the registration process with Iowa State Board of Mortuary Science, correct?"

"I am."

"Mandy, let's sit at this table."

They sat across from each other at a small oval table in his office.

"Fill me in on your family, your husband."

Mandy shared that her parents were good, working hard as always. Then she mentioned Owen's dad and his being in the hospital in Des Moines, for an aortic valve replacement. Owen basically now would take over the farm operation.

"For you, and also, let Owen know, we're hoping all goes well with Brad's operation. I'm told the recovery takes time."

"Five to eight weeks, and he cannot drive until the doc says it's OK."

"You left us over three years ago, Mandy. We remember your work ethic and your empathy for the grieving. What I always marveled at," he smiled to her, "was your positive approach to your work. You'll admit that distress and depression, well you saw that day after day from our clients. But you never let it get you down. I've talked to the Danier Mortuary. They totally approved of your work and said we'd be lucky to get you back. The same great recommendation came from your mortuary science instructors." He paused, "We want you to work for us. However."

Mandy heard the trigger word and thought, "Oh, here it comes, God stay with me."

She continued to sit up very straight with her back not quite touching the chair. She held her hands in her lap and looked straight ahead, maintaining eye contact with Tom.

"Much's happened in the mortuary business in the last few years, especially since you left us for school. During the downturn some mortuaries did not make it. Kristy and I made a decision to become part of a very large network of mortuaries. With that change came changes for us. You saw the revamping of the chapel, the reception area, and outside. Plus there've been updates of our equipment and the whole venue with the corpse."

Tom stopped and collected his thoughts. He began again.

"We can offer you a 4/5ths position, (32 hours) as is the suggested start with this mortuary corporation of which we are now a part. You qualify for medical, 401K, and after two years, the possibility of stock options. We aren't a little operation any more, Mandy. We're part of a large North American network of mortuaries. I know you'd talked to us years ago about one day buying us out. That option is no longer available. We're a big business now."

"Still the only mortuary in Porttown?"

"Correct, one other started up, but was gone within a year. There are many regulations involving the whole funeral industry. You learned about those in your studies."

Mandy nodded to him and asked about the starting salary. He gave her the figure, told her that there were sixth month and one year reviews of her work, a standard from the corporation. They discussed salary raises, which would come with reviews.

"Is there a chance I'll be full-time one day?"

"Every possibility, but not until after at least a year for us to see how you get along."

"I accept your offer to work with you, to help the bereaved, to prepare the loved one for the next stage. I am glad to be back."

Tom and Mandy stood and shook hands.

"We'll have your paperwork ready in a day or so, signing off on your 401 K and medical."

"And we'd like you to start next Monday. We'll have you begin in the business office, learning our national's way of doing things. I'm certain our procedures vary a little from what you did at Danier."

Mandy nodded, smiled to him and asked him to say hello to Kristy. On her way out she stopped at the business office and said hello to the receptionist and bookkeeper. She knew both women from her working there three years ago. They asked, so she shared that she took the job, returning to work with them.

"Welcome aboard, we're so glad you're back. Young people here, that's gonna be helpful, 'cause we're all getting older," Beth shared.

Mandy looked at the two of them, "Well, so am I," she giggled and got them to laugh.

She made an appointment to sign off on all her paperwork for Hoskisson Mortuary. She started home. On the way she made a turn.

"Gran, I need to talk to you." After she parked along the road leading to the grave, she spoke up, "Goodness, have I forgotten where your gravestone is?"

She wandered around for a little while, then finally found an angel statue close to gran's grave. She touched the top of the gravestone, then knelt in front of it.

"Gran, it's good to be here. You know I talk to you other places, but here's where your earthly remains are. I've worked so hard for the last few years. And I can tell you I'm disappointed at my salary, and my hours. Working 32 hours means I might not be lead on any family projects for awhile. But, gran, I know I'll work some weeks, a lot more than the 32, when we have a death that we gotta deal with. And my hours, it'll be a rough first six months. The good news is, Owen's here, and I don't have to study every second.

We have a lovely home, that needs lots of work, and no yard, but the native grass, it'll be OK. I'm rambling, but I only had a few minutes with you, putting the wreath here at Christmas, 'cause I wore your dress the next day. Did you like what we did with your dress? It turned out so great. Thank you for saving it for me. It was a sweet wedding, with a super reception at our home. Hey, you know that, just need to talk. I don't know why, but I miss you right now. I'm sure it's 'cause I'm coming off a high of working so hard, a successful internship, then, wham, reality hits with my working life starting.   I love you. Owen's dad, I'm praying for him, surgery, hope he'll get better."

She got up and wiped off her knees from the dried grass she knelt in.

"Don't back down from who you are and what you want to be, gran, thank you for saying that. Sometimes over the last three years I whispered that over many times a day. It got me through some rough stuff. And God, you were right there with me," Mandy spoke out.

She turned and walked back to her car. She turned once again to gaze at her gran's grave.

"I sorta expected you to be standing there, waving to me," Mandy thought.

But there was no gran.

"I'm a big, grownup girl, now, on my own."

As she opened her car door, a poof of wind circled her. She smiled to herself and nodded her head.

"Where've I been? The dirt road into our home, it's smoother and a lot wider, enough room for two cars to pass.

And Owen, he's started putting up the rail fence, wow.   My gosh, he's done a lot that I didn't even see 'til now."

She drove into the garage and gathered her paperwork to fill out for her benefits with the mortuary.   With a burst of energy she found the paint for the guest bedroom. She painted that room a very pale blue, white with a blue tinge, a color she picked out.   Owen had the room ready for her, small stepladder for the higher walls, paper to protect the wood floor, and the paint brushes and roller and pan.

"Thank you, Owen, I can tell you've done a bunch of painting. You knew what I needed."

She remembered him saying the basement bedroom was ready for paint.   Before she headed down there with her painting supplies she checked the rest of the first floor. She saw that Owen painted the third bedroom, the same color as their bedroom.   Once down in the basement she looked around. He also painted the large basement room. Mandy peeked into the bedroom and saw that it needed painting. She saw a note attached to the paint.

"OK if you paint it the same color as the upstairs bedroom?"

"Heck ya, he saved this for me. He must'a known I'd go to work pretty much right away. Did he paint the bathroom?"

She looked in and saw it was the same color as the two upstairs bathrooms.

"When'd he have time? I bet he just did all this, helping me, he musta known I'd start work soon."

She ran up the steps to the main floor and made herself a sandwich for eating when she finished one wall. Mandy fixed a pot of coffee, took a big drink and carried a thermos down with her food.   By 10:30 she decided to stop, with just two walls left.

"What'll I do tomorrow afternoon?"

She decided she would sleep on it. And she knew Owen would call, to let her know about the surgery.   The next morning she awoke to bright sunshine. She fixed herself a big breakfast, ate it, and drank two cups of coffee. She cleaned up and went to the basement.

Mandy looked around at the bedroom after she turned on the lights. She saw places on the wall which she immediately repainted.

"I musta been super tired by the end of the night, couldn't see the difference between the white and the pale blue."

She ran upstairs for one final slug of coffee, then returned to the basement and painted the final two walls. She heard her cell ring from near the door of the bedroom.

"Owen, what's up?"

"Dad's surgery, successful, I've given blood, so has mom. I'm staying on, one more night with mom. Then I'm coming home. When the docs release him, I'll go back and get them. Check their home, please, trash needs to go out to the road for tomorrow."

"I'll also check the frig, to see what they might need, you know, bread, milk."

"Thank you, Mandy, so much. I love you."

"I love you, Owen, please hug your mom and let your folks both know that they are in my thoughts and prayers."

An hour later Mandy let herself in to the Northwood home. She opened the frig and smelled it.

"Spoiled milk, and a partial meal, rotting in the frig, and the overfull trash sack, under the sink, ick," she spoke out as she emptied several other items from the refrigerator.

She went from room to room, collecting trash. After she got everything bagged up, she visited the garage. The trash can was partly full; she could hardly lift it. After three trips to the road, the first with the trash can, she finally had all the trash ready for the trash man tomorrow.

When she returned to the home, she cleared the kitchen table of dishes and opened the dishwasher. It was stacked full of dirty dishes. She looked at the time on the stove clock. She shook her head and started the dishwasher. Then she hand washed and dried the dishes and pans from breakfast the day his parents left for Des Moines.

"It's not like Sara to leave a mess. Oh, Mandy, don't be so critical, she's got a sick husband, and the house's obviously not on her mind. Get a grip, and help out; oh dear, it's comin' back to me. I did the same thing at gran's, after she died, the trash, the kitchen clean up," she nodded her head as reminder tears came to her eyes.

She made a list of what she needed to accomplish before Monday of next week. Tomorrow she had to sign up for her medical insurance and her 401K and get groceries for Owen's parents and them. What about the yard? She shook her head and knew that Owen would help her with that. She added dinners to invite folks to, for her folks, and for Owen's parents.

And she asked, "I wonder if we might get away for a weekend, a tiny honeymoon, one of these months before harvest?"

She emptied the dishwasher, putting away as many of the dishes and pans as she could remember locations, when she helped out in Sara's kitchen.

"Nice," she looked around, smelling a cleaner kitchen.

She trudged along the trail that crossed through the trees from his parents' home to their home

"I sure need You, God, I can't yank myself outa this funk. I had so much joy, so looking forward to my returning here. Hey, I've got a job. Will it take time?"

She stopped talking, really wanting a response. She heard quiet, God's response.

"I have a wonderful home; I'll try to make it a place of comfort and love," she spoke out as she let herself in the front door. "Owen'll come home tomorrow. God, I have so much to be thankful for. And yes, feeling more positive will take time. Did I expect too much?"

7

2013

"This's grand, Mandy, having dinner outside. I hope we can do that often."

"Everything tastes good out in the fresh air, that's for sure."

"Agree; I've done all the talking since I got home."

"You have a lot on your mind; your dad, getting better, every day, that's the most important thing."

"Right, let's gather everything up and head in. Soon, it'll be so humid and buggy, out here."

They took in their plates and put the chairs close to the small circle table on the back patio. He helped her clean up.

"You wanted to show me what you've done."

"Uh huh."

She showed him the guest bedroom.

"Wow, the pale color turned out nice, and I think we did a good job of picking out the bedspread, sheets, and pillowcases. You got these all washed up and on the bed, thanks."

She took him to the basement. He looked into the bedroom.

"Nice, it's the same color as the one bedroom you just painted upstairs, but the light gives it a tiny lavender hue. We'll figure something out for furniture in this room, maybe a double bed against the wall, so it can be like a couch by day."

He followed her from the bedroom and stood next to her as they gazed around the large room.

"Man cave, Owen," Mandy hugged him.

"Maybe, a little football watching down here, with a flat screen. There's a small flat screen in the great room; it isn't interfering with the fireplace. The fireplace, for sure is the focal point of the room."

"I agree."

"Mandy, you been super busy since you got home, my gosh, have you slept much?"

"Troubled."

"Let's talk later; I need to call mom to see how dad is. You been in touch with your folks?"

"Just to let them know I got a job at the mortuary; they seemed pleased. I really appreciated that they didn't ask me about my salary."

"Yeah, it's actually none of their business."

She nodded as she smiled to him, "I love you, and you so understand. How'd you get to be so doggone smart."

"Dunno, just come and kiss me, baby," he said in his Owen-special drawl.

He took her hand after she gave him a deep French kiss. They drifted into their bedroom.

An hour later they tossed on sweatshirts and shorts and returned to the kitchen for dessert.

Mandy put a dish of his favorite chocolate chip ice cream and sugar cookies in front of him. She sat next to him starting in on her own dessert.

"My first dessert, wunerful Mandy, and this dessert," he paused and gave her a kiss on her cheek, "this dessert is nice."

She turned to him, "But, not like the first."

"Right," he winked to her.

They took decaf coffee to the new sectional in the great room.

She drank her coffee and began.

"Think you can tell, I got a lot on my mind."

"Right."

She shared her salary with Owen, and that for many weeks there would be many more than 32 hours in her work week. It would be nights when the mortuary needed to pick up a body from the morgue, or from a hospital in another town.

"You did that at your internship mortuary?"

"We did, indeed, three different times."

"So your first six months, they'll be kinda a 24/7 situation."

"Exactly."

"But now I know what that's actually going to mean for you, getting up in the middle of the night to go in."

"It's the reality of what I'll be doing. But that won't be that often."

"It will be what it will be."

"Thank you for understanding that. I'm not working a Monday to Friday, 8 to 5 kinda occupation. The money's not that good; it'll get better as time and my reviews go by. And that makes me really uneasy, Owen."

"Why uneasy?"

She stopped and refreshed both their coffees.

"Two things, remember how I used to talk about buying out Tom and Kristy and taking over the mortuary as my own business?"

"For sure, tell me what's going on."

"Hoskisson's is part of a very large mortuary corporation now. Tom, I think, realized that the business might be more than they wanted to attempt as they aged. Anyway they bought into the whole corporation situation, so not really a buyout opportunity. Tom and I talked that over when I agreed to take the job, when we discussed salary and benefits. Like I've asked myself over and over again, did I expect too much, getting started, and not one day being able to take over?"

"Time, Mandy, I think you'll be surprised, and maybe one day, you'll manage the whole mortuary situation at Hoskisson's. That may be enough to satisfy you. I know you want to rush, but it's a one day at a time situation, like dad."

"Thanks for your input, but there's a second thing," she looked into his brown eyes. "I'm very uneasy; I'm not contributing that much to our total economic situation. Owen, you've never shared with me where you got the money to build our home. You haven't asked me for a dime, but I want to contribute."

"OK, I'll share this, corn crops, money I've saved, money my folks set aside for a four year college education, and my salary with the Guard. And Mandy, you had to get all your schooling paid for, which you've done."

"Still, I want to help. What can I do?"

"Work, put some of your salary into a joint checking account we need to set up. Everything's been separate, has had to be separate, with us living in two different locations, actually you were in three for a time. We need to work this out over time. You're very conscientious."

"And I try to be frugal."

"You are that."

"So, I'll continue to stress out about stuff, until I'm really on my feet and helping out. In the meantime, you got your dad to deal with. That's gotta be #1."

"It will be, and I know you'll help out my folks."

"Like you asked me, I dealt with the trash, ran the dishwasher and cleaned up the kitchen in your folks' home. Your mom's very neat, usually. I could tell she was stressed to the max before leaving with your dad to Des Moines."

"Yeah, sometimes mom doesn't say much, but I know stuff's zooming around in her head, especially about dad. I can tell you that she's come to me several times in the last few months, thanking me for learning everything I can about the farm operation. She definitely doesn't want to have to deal with the farm should something happen to dad."

"Sara's talked to me a bit about several changes in the homestead. I gave her suggestions, what little I know."

"Yeah, she'll get bathrooms remodeled and the kitchen changed a bit. That's coming real soon."

"I think that's a great idea, while your dad can be around to help a little, or offer suggestions."

"Uh huh, he'll go nuts not being able to be outside, working, and getting ready for harvest, but that won't be for a few months."

"Oh," she paused and looked out the window, "our yard, Owen, what do you want to do?"

"Front, let's keep it in the native grass, just keep it mowed and watered, if necessary, which I haven't been doing; maybe a tree, that doesn't get too big to dwarf the home. And the back, that's up to you, a little garden, flowers, more native grass."

"What about wild flowers?"

"Sounds great, it's up to you. Let's see what happens as you get into your work mode."

"I'm getting tired; oh, I really like the rail fence you're putting up on both sides of the driveway."

"I'm glad; I thought you'd be pleased," he kissed her on the cheek and took their coffee cups to the sink.

℘

"Sally, what do you think?"

"It's wonderful, what Owen's done on this land and with this home. Subcontracting work out, and getting folks to help, he's created a place of love and peace for the two of you."

Mandy got a call from her girlhood friend the week before Mandy returned to Porttown. They agreed to meet at Mandy's new home on the Sunday before Mandy went to work at the mortuary. Sally arrived early afternoon and brought special coffee she thought Mandy and Owen would enjoy.

Owen worked outside on the rail fence as the women took their coffee to the back patio. Mandy shared her feelings about her internship now that she graduated and got ready for the real world of death and bereavement.

"This is so the perfect occupation for you, Mandy. And you've known that for a very long time."

"It was gran; she's my reason for pursuing my field of work, what I learned, from her, and after she died."

Mandy looked at Sally and shook her head as she looked into Sally's veined red eyes.

"You gotta share, girlfriend. Your eyes, you seem not quite yourself." She paused, "'cept we've been apart for three years. I know you couldn't come to the wedding, so talk to me."

"I'm a junior credit wise at Northern Iowa, and I want to be with teens. So I'm in the secondary teaching concentration, math and science."

"That's great for you," Mandy paused and touched Sally's shoulder, "I know about STEM, how we need girls to be in the science and math venues. You'll be a great example to girls, with that kinda background."

"Hope so, I'm a mess now. I'm getting help at the university counseling center. I started drinking, heavy drinking, at last Thanksgiving. I didn't come home for a few months. Drinking led to sex, and sex led to a pregnancy. Three different guys, three different nights, no protection. Out of my mind with passion, all alcohol induced; can you believe that, Mandy?"

Mandy watched the tears dribble down Sally's cheeks.

"Judge not, Mandy, judge not," her inner voice screamed.

"With all that alcohol over those three days, I finally got good and sick to my stomach. For several days after that, I just took a headache pill, and drank tons of water until I could keep food down. I'm not drinking at all now. I saw first-hand what could happen. So with the pregnancy, I had an abortion. And now I'm grieving the death of the baby I gave up. I'm angry, at myself, sad, crying a lot, I gotta go on, it's helping to talk this out with you."

"Oh, Sally, I'm so sorry for your loss."

She came around and hugged Sally.

After she sat back down Mandy said, "We gotta talk to each other more often. What can I do to help you?"

"What you're doing now, listening."

"Please keep talking to your counselor at school. That's what you need to do for me, Sally. It won't be long before you'll intern, in a high school, finding out if working with teens is what you'll really want. Like I just finished my internship in April. We have to test the waters, to know if we'll be able to swim through the deep waves as well as the shallow waters."

Sally started smiling to Mandy.

"Exactly, I've been in deep waters in my personal life, now I'll work on my professional life. Oh, Mandy, you make good sense."

She watched as Sally's eyes brightened for the first time in their conversation.

"You'll be so good with the sad folks who've just lost someone. I know, you've just cheered me up."

"One day at a time, Sally, it's what I tell my bereaved families. Today's all we got, girlfriend."

"Yeah, past is passed, and future, unknown, except for the little stuff we can try to do."

"Exactly."

"Mandy, do you think God will ever forgive me, for giving someone permission to kill the fetus in me?"

"I can't answer that; God is loving, He loves you and He loves me. Have you thought about talking to a religious person?"

"I guess I need to try that, hey, I gotta go. I'm getting along really good with my folks right now. And your folks, and Owen's?"

"My folks," she gave Sally a wide-eyed look, "seemed genuinely glad I graduated, but there's still that we'll-see attitude they've always had about what I want to do with my life. And Owen's folks, I love them to pieces, awesome folks. Brad just had heart surgery, and is on the mend."

"That mean Owen's taken over?"

"Pretty much."

"It's what he's wanted, all along."

"Right."

Sally helped bring in the cups. Mandy walked her to her car.

"Thank you for taking the time to come out here."

"We'll renew our friendship, Mandy. I hope one day to teach here in Iowa."

They stood at Sally's car.

"I love you, Sally."

"And I love you, Mandy, please say hello to Owen."

They hugged.

"I will, God bless and keep you, Sally."

"You also."

Mandy saw her friend smile.

�

"I love you so much, Mandy."

"And I love you, am over the moon for you, Owen."

They spoke that as they held hands, walking through the snow at Landview. Owen carried the evergreen wreath in his other hand. He handed the long wreath to Mandy.

"Gran, Happy Christmas. I don't remember if I did this last Christmas. It was such a crazy time in my life. But Owen and I, we're back to brighten your gravestone."

Mandy bent down and brushed snow from the front of the gravestone.

She rose up, "This year I put little red berries and small pinecones in your wreath, stuff that reminds me of nature, and of you."

Together Owen and Mandy lay the wreath in front of the gravestone.

"Gran, it's been quite a time for us."

"My dad, he's feeling lots better, aortic valve replacement, and he's almost back to his old self. I've kinda taken over. Dad's relieved, and mom, well, she's really happy."

"Gran, I've completed six months at the mortuary. And I've had my review. I'm pleased. I'll have another at one year. We're really busy; there're more older folks in Porttown, than ever before. So there're more deaths. It's the ebb and flow of life."

They held hands as they walked through the snow to the road and their car.

"What's left for us to do about Christmas dinner?"

"Everybody's helping; Granddad Overton's driving in for dinner and spending the night with us."

"He'll be our first guest in the basement bedroom."

"Yeah, I'll be anxious to hear how he likes it down there; he's got a window in his bedroom, so that will bring in light. And he's got the bathroom, which has hardly ever been used."

As they drove home, Owen turned to her, "How does it seem that your granddad is getting along with your parents?"

"Very well, you understand, they can never know, correct?"

"That's correct; that seemed so long ago when we sat together and you had me read those letters from your granddad to your gran."

"It was a long time ago."

"You're happy, about your family, how're they relating?"

"Never dreamed dad and his dad, well, God takes care of us all."

"Right."

That night they attended midnight service with Owen's parents and meemaw. So many life snapshots swirled in Mandy's head as she stood and sat through the ceremony with them. The service, the year gran died, it stood out the most. She remembered the beautiful music, sitting next to her brother, Michael. The music touched her heart as well as her ears. Since that time holiday music filled her with joy and peace.

Granddad Overton drove in Christmas morning. He brought champagne, to celebrate Owen and Mandy's first anniversary.

"Granddad," Mandy smiled to him as she showed him his bedroom and bathroom, "you're our very first guest in our home, so we welcome you."

"It's so great to be with you and Owen. I hadn't been invited away from my place for many years."

"Uncle Justin?"

"Coping, he's not done the grieving he should have, after his mom died, and after we found out about the baby's death."

He took a deep breath, in and out.

"Only you understand this, Mandy, we don't know which of us is the father of the baby."

They stood together in the bedroom. Mandy turned and hugged her granddad. He returned her hug as his tears started.

"Granddad, did you get help, a counselor, after all this happened?"

"I did, but not until a couple of years ago, so I suffered, I know now, needlessly."

"Grief, recovery, it all takes time."

They let go of each other.

"Don't mean to preach, but you, and me, and all of us, we're God's children; and he loves us all, those who died early, and he loves all of us, who are alive today. So baby Stanton, that's the baby, that baby is loved by God. It's what we can hold on to, God's love for us."

"Thank you Mandy, I know you do a wonderful job, are a counselor to all your grieving folks."

"I help them through the initial grieving, but some must get other counseling, from professionals, to go on."

"Thank you, Mandy, Happy Christmas, let's head up and celebrate with the family."

Mandy's folks drove in before the noon meal, and Brad and Sara Northwood walked across the trail from the homestead. They each carried food, Sara a pumpkin pie and whipped cream, and Brad the herb stuffing.

Mandy baked a ham and a turkey breast with gravy. And her folks brought a potato dish. Owen baked rolls.

"Mandy, oh Mandy, look, wow, the rolls are golden brown on the bottom. Are you proud of me, not burning the bottoms?"

She kissed him on the lips and nodded, "Very impressed, I declare you my for-real assistant chef."

The family stood near them

"Did you, did you hear that," he looked around at the family with wide eyes, "my dear darling Mandy declares me assistant chef."

Mandy heard the claps and cheers and one piercing whistle for her Owen. He hugged Mandy. Several times during the meal Mandy felt tears in her eyes.

"I'm so happy," she whispered to Owen as they served dessert.

"I also feel that way, our family together, except Michael and Matt."

As Mandy took her last bite of pie, she looked across to her granddad and meemaw.

"Thank you God, for having Owen and me descend from these folks, our grandparents," she thought and said a silent prayer.

ॐ

"Want to show you, our field out back of our home, Mandy, show you how the fields are planted, the thought this year."

They put on their heavy coats and serious boots and trudged through the snow to the back field.

"On this late Christmas afternoon, here's what we do."

Owen walked, held out his arms, "So, here to here, that's the corn, then in the middle between each planted row of corn, we plant alfalfa. It helps protect the corn, you know, the pesky bugs. On the next field we plant soybeans. We rotate crops every year."

"Some years do you keep a field or two fallow?"

"We do, to resurrect the soil, bring back its mineral content."

"So, you, Owen, are really a researcher, finding the best way to handle the corn."

"Yep, now you know, sorry I hadn't explained that before."

"The soil, the moisture, the effort, it's all so marvelous, and it's life repeating itself, year after year. It's so refreshing, what you do."

"Thank you, missy, I know you appreciate what my work is."

ॐ

"Michael's been in a car accident. They want us there, Mandy. We're not sure how bad it is."

Mandy stood in the kitchen, on her way out the door to work. She held the cell phone in one hand and set down her cup of coffee.

"I'm so sorry, Dad, going by car?"

"Yeah, 'cause Mom and I don't know how long we'll be there; gas for the trip and using our own car's better than flying and getting a rental."

"Uh, not sure, where is he right now?"

"Wright Patterson, on assignment there, a TDY, so he's at Wright Pat's medical facility."

"So Iowa to Ohio."

"Right, the weather's holding at the moment."

"We'll keep Michael, you and mom, in our thoughts and prayers."

"That's all we can do, thanks, Mandy."

"You'll keep us informed."

"Uh huh, gotta go."

"God bless and keep you and mom."

ℂ

At 6:30 the next morning, three weeks after the holidays, Mandy's cell rang. She always kept it on, because her job remained 24/7, a call at any time to pick up a body from a location to the mortuary.

"Mandy?"

"Granddad, are you OK? Hey, talk to me."

She heard her granddad's sobs.

"Mandy, I need your help."

"Start slow, and tell me everything."

She grabbed paper and pencil and began writing as her granddad spoke.

"Got a call an hour ago, from the sheriff in your county. I need you to identify your Uncle Justin at the coroner's office. From what the sheriff said, he committed suicide, in his car, on a country road outside Porttown. There was a note. I think he was coming to see his brother."

"Did you know dad and mom are at a hospital at Wright Pat; Michael's been in a car accident?   The hospital wanted them there; don't know how bad Michael is."

"No, I didn't know about the accident. All I know is that Justin told me in our last conversation that he wanted to talk to his brother, after all this time, kinda to get back together."

"Of course, Granddad, Owen and I will head to the coroner's office to identify him. You know my job; I'll make sure Justin's body gets transferred to Hoskisson's. That's my duty right now, body pickup and delivery."

"Mandy, the sheriff said he basically shot his neck off. You should be able to identify him because he looks basically the same as the last time you saw him."

"Got it, Granddad; don't come, we'll keep talking and get this worked out. I know he's a family member, but I'm so used to doing this kind of stuff."

"I love you, Mandy, and I know you are not insensitive; you've learned to work with death as you work with life for the survivors."

Mandy set the phone on the counter and turned. Owen stood near her. He took her in his arms and held her tight. Her eyes teared, and she felt one quick pain in the area of her heart.

"How much of that did you pick up, Owen?"

"Most everything, I am so sorry, Mandy. I suspect he never stopped grieving for the baby that might have been his, of a different life he might have had."

"Exactly, let's see what the suicide note says."

Owen drove them to the facility. They got escorted into the coroner's area. Owen gripped Mandy's hand as the coroner lifted the sheet.

"Yes, that's my Uncle Justin, Justin Overton," she whispered, then spoke out louder a second time.

They visited the Sheriff's Office next.

"Thank you for identifying and claiming the body, Mandy. You've been in here several times the last few months, right?"

Mandy told the deputy about her work at Hoskisson's.

"That's right, I thought I recognized you."

"His father, my granddad, asked me to retrieve the note and get the car pulled out of impound, when it's available. I'll be by later today with a helper to remove my uncle's body. I'm making the decision for granddad, to have Uncle Justin cremated. And the gun, do what you will with it. I know granddad doesn't want the weapon back."

Mandy thanked the sheriff's office for their assistance. She always did that as she left, but this time it was personal.

"I'm taking you to our little place for an early lunch."

"Thanks, Owen, I'll call in to get a time and a helper to bring Justin back to the mortuary."

"Holy cripes, Mandy, you are so tough."

"Yeah, this is a regular work day for me, except this is a family member. I don't have an emotional attachment to him, except maybe the heartache he caused gran. Remember, I go to hospitals, homes, accident sites, wherever we're asked to retrieve someone's loved one."

They sat in their little favorite cafe, sharing a chocolate milkshake, a favorite of Mandy's, in addition to toasted cheese sandwiches, curly fries, and coffee.

"Owen, do you think granddad will want Justin buried next to his mom, at Landview?"

"Uh, maybe, think so; what can I do?"

"Go home, do your stuff, call Landview, they'll be able to tell you if there's a place next to gran; of yeah, she's Mary Beth Stanton, on her gravestone."

"I remember."

"Thanks for finding out what you can; we'll call and talk to granddad tonight. I told him not to come. He's gonna freak out when he finds out how much it costs to cremate Justin. And he's gotta take care of Justin's estate; I doubt he had a will, and he'll have to clear Justin's place. Thanks God, that Justin just rented, no property to deal with, except his personal stuff."

"I know you musta seen some real disasters with the money issues at a death."

"You can imagine how upset the survivors are, the death, plus the death's cost."

"Oh Mandy, I'm just starting to get a grip on everything you guys do at the mortuary, the body, well, that's just one piece of everything that happens."

"Uh huh, pretty incredible, it sure was for me, until I got used to the whole situation. Funeral service work, it's service work, just like your Guard service, and of course, the corn crop."

"I gotta get you to the mortuary. I'll pick you up, when you call me. I want to show you about how the crops get planted, maybe in the next day or so."

"Uh, actual planting's in April?"

"Right."

֍

"We are so sorry about your uncle, Mandy."

Kristy Hoskisson hugged Mandy as she came into her office.

"Are you sure you want to do pickup?"

"Absolutely, Kristy, I identified him earlier. So it won't be a shock to see him again. I'll talk to granddad, but we need to do an immediate cremation."

"I'll alert the crematory and will make certain your uncle goes in tomorrow."

"Good, I'm sure my granddad wants an immediate resolution. Owen's working with Landview. Granddad can decide on a monument, to come later."

֍

"Hey, pizza tonight, but it's Monday, not Friday."

"Yeah, Owen darlin', it's been a day, got Justin delivered to the crematory."

"So, to help cheer you up, it's pizza time again."

"How did the conversation go with your granddad?"

"He said several expletives after I shared the cost of a cremation with a cardboard box. Uh, and then he apologized."

"Hey, when I have to tell him about the cost of the gravesite, next to gran, he'll be upset again."

"But Owen, since Justin's cremated, there is no rush to put him in a grave. It can wait, for a time, until granddad recovers."

"You guys, can keep the ashes, at Hoskisson's?"

"Right, we do that, 'cept we don't have many cremations. In this part of the U.S. folks still like the ceremony, the casket, the service, the reception, just like what I'll continue to do."

"Final thing, with granddad, he'll have to deal with Justin's vehicle, in impound, you told him that?"

"I did."

Owen cut the pizza and they sat at the kitchen island, savoring the three-meat pizza, with cheese-filled crust. They finished off their meal with chocolate ice cream.

"I'm starting to get sad, Owen."

"Yeah, you gotta tell your dad when he calls. I sure hope Michael's gonna be OK."

"God's in charge. Thank you for being there for me today, and now you see what I do, not sitting in an office very much of the time."

Owen leaned to Mandy and kissed her cheek.

Mandy's call from her dad only took several minutes. She went to the couch and sat next to Owen.

"All he said about Justin was 'I'm so sorry.' They'll be home day after tomorrow. They're moving Michael to a rehab hospital for a few days. He's got a broken leg, had to have a pin put in it, looks like permanent. Once he's on his feet he'll go back to work on crutches."

"Sure glad God's got a plan; I couldn't 'a predicted that one."

"Me neither."

"First year, married, Mandy, it's been a wild and crazy back and forth time."

"Maybe it won't settle down, like Justin and Michael."

"Gotta say, it's been mighty interesting."

"Maybe, in two weeks, I'll check to see if I'm on retrieval duty that weekend, if I'm not, let's get away, Owen."

"I can tell you sure need a break from all this, Mandy."

"Yeah, just a couple of days, a change of scenery."

"Mandy, go get the note; it's important that we read it, and then let your granddad know. I think I kinda know what he wrote."

Mandy went to their bedroom and opened the bottom drawer of a chest, where she still kept precious items from her life. She brought it to the couch.

"Read it to yourself, Owen, please."

He read and passed the note to her.

Sadness for her uncle caught Mandy up. Tears spurted from her eyes and the knot of grief she felt in her throat moved up into her nose as she read.

I'm meeting my baby; I'm claiming this little one as my own. I'm going home, really going home, to mom. I've caused her unbelievable sadness, and I'm so sorry.

"We need to keep this, Mandy, in case."

"Granddad needs to read it."

"He does, but I think that he doesn't want your dad reading it."

"Do you think dad will ever even ask?"

"Dunno, you mean to see it?"

"Yeah."

"It will accomplish nothing. What went on, is between your gran, granddad, and uncle. But we know."

"Owen, like we said those years ago, we take it to our grave."

"We do."

℅

"This's been a grand weekend, Owen."

"I wanted it to be special, since next week'll be a tough one for you."

Owen took Mandy to Des Moines, for a Friday and Saturday night in a downtown hotel, with room service for breakfast Saturday morning. They went to a pub the night before for food and sodas.

"How awesome, breakfast in bed, with my sweet wonderful guy."

"It's a very short, very belated honeymoon."

"But we'll have several more."

They ate, set the food aside, and made love. Later they went out to early dinner and a play.

Late that night they lay side by side after lovemaking. Owen gave her a tiny box. She opened it and found a small golden angel.

"I give this little angel to you with love, small but precious," he whispered.

"Oh Owen, I will wear it, every day, on the lapel of my suit jacket, a little angel to guide me, as God guides me. Thank you, you are so thoughtful; it is a welcomed present."

She kissed him and they embraced each other.

☙

They held hands as they walked up the steps to the Stanton home. They celebrated Christmas at home earlier in the day. Mandy's parents asked her granddad, meemaw, and Owen's folks for a 2 p.m. Christmas dinner. Owen carried a sack of rolls he baked himself. Everyone wanted to see how his second year of Christmas baking turned out. Mandy held a can of cranberry sauce. Cindy asked for that to go with the turkey she prepared.

"Another year, Mandy, unbelievable, how fast time's sprinting on."

"A fine Christmas holiday, with Michael able to join us."

Mandy heard Christmas music in the background as the family dug in to the turkey dinner. The conversation remained light, everyone telling a humorous tale from a previous Christmas in their lives.

After the meal and cleanup Granddad Stanton came to Mandy.

"Sweetie, you seem tired, your eyes not so bright."

She looked into his eyes, "Uh huh, I am, was on body retrieval, at one o'clock this morning, from a home just outside of town."

"To the coroner's office?"

"Right, and then the mortuary'll handle the rest."

"There is no holiday in your business."

She nodded to him, "No, there is not. But up above, it's Christmas in heaven, so joy's there."

He hugged her and thanked her for letting him spend Christmas night with Owen and her.

The next morning the family assembled at Landview.

Time, this one year later, helped soothe the pain of Justin's suicide for the Overton family. Jim set his brother's ashes in the opened gravesite. Mandy brought a bouquet of several colors of roses. Each family member picked a rose for the grave, spoke a quiet remembrance and dropped in the rose. Owen and Mandy remained at the grave for a few minutes after everyone else returned to their cars.

"Owen?"

"Ask me."

"I look too much at everything around me, in the distance and close in. It's something I started doing at gravesites, because a person just never knows about the families and friends of the dead person. And I noticed, today, way in the distance, a tall person in a long black coat, and it looked like a head covering of some sort. The person, I think a woman, stood for a time as we gathered. Then when I looked up the person was gone. I did not see the leaving. Am I seeing figures, who aren't there?"

"I feel confident you did see someone, someone who took the time to come to this place, maybe to honor Justin."

"Do you think it could be?"

Owen looked at her, with her wide smile and questioning eyes.

"That's possible."

He touched her shoulder.

"What I do know is that I love you, Mandy."

"I love you, Owen."

"And I can't believe how strong you are," he gazed at her, "to carry on, to finish what needed to happen for Justin, your own family. He was a child of God, just as we all are."

"This's what I do," she looked up into Owen's brown eyes and nodded, "what I'll always do as I continue to help folks recover from a loved one's death."

They stood and gave each other a soft caressing kiss. Mandy and Owen held hands as they walked toward their family, who stood, waiting for them.

CHRISTMAS BRIGHT

Book One in the Jenny/Ann Trilogy

19-year-old Madison falls in love with a widower, David, in this prequel to Baskets on Christmas Lane. She teaches and becomes a stepmother to David's young daughter, Jenny, after they marry. An avalanche kills David days after their son, Christopher, is born.

Madison adjusts to life as a single parent, while still teaching. She and Jenny grieve for David. Her dad, John, moves to the ski town of Happy Valley, CO to help Madison. An outing of skiing with Jenny and Christopher brings Madison face to face with Todd. That Christmas Eve Madison invites Todd to her home. As they spend time together, they discover a strong passion for each other.

Suspicious circumstances regarding the avalanche that killed David are revealed. Madison and Todd marry, after being away from each other for a while. Christopher and Jenny love their new dad. The family moves to Hickam Air Force Base,

Hawaii. Their son, Seth, is born. Todd continues to advance in his Air Force career causing several moves for their family.

Time passes. Jenny works with young people as a student teacher in music. Christopher attends the U.S. Naval Academy; Seth is in high school. Madison continues as an English teacher. The family faces a terrible crisis when Jenny disappears without a trace. A private investigator takes over this cold case with no success.

In her whole heart and mind, Madison believes that Jenny survives, that God watches over her. On a Christmas Eve in their home at Andrews Air Force Base, Madison receives a cassette tape. She shares the tape with her family. It brings them joy, and hope.

ABOUT CATHLEEN

WWW.CATHLEENELLIS.COM

Cathleen Ellis is a Colorado native. She and her husband, John, live in the northern part of the state. They have four sons, three daughters-in-law, and four grandchildren. Cathleen draws the inspiration for her love stories from the lives of young people with whom she has lived and worked her entire life.